I0615401

**Beloved Readers Share Their Love for
K. W. LEONE**

"A book that takes you on a journey. An experience in and of itself. A fresh view on the fantasy genre with character bonds that leave a lasting impression. You'll find yourself falling in love with the world, and not wanting to put the book down." - Jayden Walker

"You'll be holding your breath on one page, only to have it stolen it away on the next! Grayden's Promise offers the continuation of an already vibrant and brilliant tale, and a journey that is far from over." - A. Hutchison

"Warmage is a trip through a world that mirrors our reality, splashing intrigue and extraordinary elements onto each page to keep the reader wanting more." - L. C.

"This book became one of my favorites very fast. As a fantasy lover it has everything I could ask for. It's magical and the world building is just brilliant. The characters feel authentic and relatable, and I keep wondering what intentions everyone might have. You also get this immense war setting with intrigues and old kingdoms and of course the outlandish enemies. I am very excited for the second volume and can't wait to figure out what the future will hold for Grayden, Tylen and the others!" -A.F.

"Tell me magic isn't dead for humans, or dragons. That we haven't broken everything? Lie to me if you have to…" Brynn's voice wavered as he trailed off into the quiet.

"I assure you that it *is* not, *has* not, and *will* not." Grayden said resolutely. "Tell me, Brynn—when you watch the aurora on cold winter nights, or when you see a beautiful bird or beast, does it still take your breath? Do you still feel wonder?"

Brynn nodded. "Yes, the first time I saw Tylen I felt that way. Or when I found myself alone on the snowy plains between Skyeford and Belden… I could feel how vast everything was, and how small I was, and that didn't scare me, it felt incredible."

Grayden could sense Tylen's eyes on him, and he couldn't help smiling through his own grief and exhaustion. "Then the dragons did their job. Magic is still alive, and some humans remember how important it is. You can't extinguish magic, because you can't kill hope."

Author K.W. Leone returns with Grayden's Promise: the second book in the LGBT+ inclusive 'Warmage' series.

Tylen had never entertained the thought of romance, let alone pursing a relationship with a human prince. As a dragon, and a runaway teenage soldier, he has bigger things to worry about. An alien invasion is tearing apart his world. The sociopolitical fallout from a centuries-old plague has come back to haunt humans and dragons alike, and a very important key has gone missing in the wake of a fiery coup.

To make matters worse, the only father-figure Tylen has ever had, Grayden, is gone—attending to a matter of grave importance. The archmage can't advise anyone, which means Brynn and Tylen need to rely on each other more than ever. But with the dark secrets of his past spilling over, Tylen has nowhere to turn. If he doesn't face the malice rooted in his history, all Anteas has fought for is lost, but if he does, he risks losing Brynn forever.

Warmage:
v.2
Grayden's Promise

Warmage:
Grayden's Promise

by:
K.W. LEONE

Copyright © 2019 by K.W.Leone

All rights reserved. No part of this book may be reproduced, scanned, or distributed in any printed or electronic form without permission.

This is a work of fiction. Names, characters, businesses, places, events, locales, and incidents are either the products of the author's imagination or used in a fictitious manner. Any resemblance to actual persons, living or dead, or actual events is purely coincidental.

Second Edition: September 2020

Printed in the United States of America

ISBN: 978-1-71655-295-3

For those who need it.
I did, too.

Acknowledgment

Many thanks to those who have supported me on this venture; from my cheerleaders and beta readers, to my editors and sensitivity consultants—I couldn't have done it without you.

Then, there is the matter of you, my reader. I cherish you. I hear you, and I see you. Every writer tells the story they needed to hear when they were young—but this tale is for you just as much as it is for me. I hope you grow to love Anteas as much as I do, and that you find a home away from home, imperfect though it may be.

Chapter One

The sheer amount of rain pouring from the sky was incredible. Skyeford's storm-frozen earth had yielded to a warm easterly front, and the land was as confused as Tylen. The young mage's hood was a sodden mass against the top of his head, and his golden hair had faded to dun straggles that trailed forlornly down the front of his robes. He was cold and miserable, and had no idea where his human charge had gone.

Between his breaths, steam continued to rise like a querulous serpent—and he shook his head at himself. He would never find Brynn in such inclement weather. As if the rain wasn't enough, a wall of fog had rolled down from the mountains, trailing its concealing hands along the ruined walls of Skyeford city. Such conditions could hide enemy motion, so he made a mental note to be cautious.

The 5th hadn't managed to recapture their home from those who had taken it, and there were still Separatists within the ravaged city that would resist anyone sporting the colors of Skyeford. They were like fleas on a dead dog, clinging until the warmth left the body; and undoubtedly, that would happen.

Before the attack Skyeford had been self-sufficient, but now that her walls were demolished, her gates splintered, and the pulse of trade had stopped... she wasn't much. Her heartbeat was her Crown, and neither king nor prince were within the city—which hadn't taken the Angelic or the Separatists long to figure out—and those who had been staunchly entrenched after the coup knew they wouldn't keep their stranglehold much longer. Figuring into this estimate, was Grayden.

The archmage was determined to take back his home, and the sorties he led had been ruthless. Skyeford hadn't been built to withstand guerrilla tactics without walls—or the fury of a mage unduly evicted. At Grayden's command, the 5th had been broken up into multiple teams that rotated between their distant barracks in the abandoned city of Helith, and the southerly Foothill Caves that housed displaced Skyeford citizens. The assault teams moved at all hours of the day from both camps, and they never struck at the same time. The level of paranoia this had induced had kept the Separatists on their toes as Grayden wore down their reserves.

It had only been a handful of weeks, but it felt longer to Tylen. Grayden had been here, there, and everywhere as was his wont; and the dragon had done his best to keep up with what was needed from both of them. Increasingly, that was to keep an eye on Brynn. Grayden had help from Sarah, his lieutenant, but Brynn effectively had no one.

Tylen liked Brynn, so the time spent with him was no real hardship—although keeping an eye on the other boy wasn't as pleasant of a task today. The weather might have been warming, but it was still wretched. Had it been anyone else, Tylen would have wondered why they insisted on being out in the elements; but considering the prince's current situation, it made perfect sense.

Brynn felt helpless, and while he was more of an observer—he always had been, unlike his father—he had reached a breaking point. Helplessness had turned to a kind of cold anger, both at himself, and the situation of his people; and he was no longer content with being paralyzed by grief. He wanted to fight. He also didn't want anyone else to be hurt, so he had made locating his father a personal crusade. This meant that he had been slipping away to search outside of the city, hoping to find some sign of the king's escape... or lack thereof.

At first the 5th had tried to dissuade Brynn, but the more they denied him, the more determined he had become. Finally, Ella, their resident tracker, had agreed to teach him her trade—if only to keep him out of trouble. Luckily, or unluckily for Tylen, the human prince was a fast study.

Today, Ella had been needed within the Foothill Caves, which meant Brynn was able to slip away unnoticed. The refugees of the caverns were busy preparing for an expedition to the Walled City, and high command had demanded Ella attend to the proceedings personally— which was wise. The 5th might have had a rogue, Donovan, in their service; but Ella's expertise as a tracker would also be a godsend, especially when it came to matters of trust.

Rogues were primarily loyal to themselves and their order, and Tylen didn't trust Donovan as far as he could throw him. High Commander Jensen seconded that sentiment—so as the situation stood, Ella was to keep an eye on Donovan, and the high commander knew she could be trusted. That didn't stop Tylen from wishing that they didn't have to keep the rogue around. He didn't trust him near Brynn. A dragon knew well enough about sellsword 'loyalty', or anyone else with Guild Republic mentality.

Since the implementation of Parliament rule, Anteas had been steadily moving towards the concept of democracy, and representation outside of Guildmasters and trade. But not all of society had caught up yet, and that led to heavy societal tension and mistrust—Especially for those from the Rogue, Healer, and Tech guilds. Unfortunately, the 5th would need someone like Donovan if they were going to find their handful of lost operatives.

The division's numbers were thin as it was, and they couldn't afford to lose any more men. Thus, as Grayden would have said, it was a 'calculated risk' to rely on a rogue. It was also their only option, and Tylen mistrusted that, too. A decision with only one choice wasn't 'deciding' anything.

Cold and frustrated, the dragon's thoughts turned back to Brynn as his glowing golden eyes scanned the ground in front of him. Even Draconic senses were muffled in this sort of weather, and he was growing increasingly concerned. No one had seen Brynn since sunrise.

Gods knew Tylen had enough to do—and other things that were nearly as important—but Skyeford's morale wouldn't survive the abduction of her Crown Prince. It was an altogether unpleasant thought, and it had grown from 'possible' to 'probable' in the dragon's mind— especially with the frequency which the prince demanded to be allowed to roam alone.

Up until the last few weeks, Tylen had prided himself on his rationality—and now he wondered if he knew anything about himself, or humans, at all. Dragons perceived emotions differently, and he was coming to understand that human feelings were, at best, endlessly nuanced. That was why his own tangled mix of sentiments kept blindsiding him. He didn't understand how he could feel love, fear, frustration, and need all at once—and if he was perfectly honest, he was afraid there was something wrong with him. Especially considering how easily distracted he had become.

Case in point, the young warmage was so absorbed in his thoughts that he didn't realize that Maylin had strode up behind him—until her warm hand dropped on his sodden shoulder. Half-turning, Tylen surprised her, and himself, by not startling or immediately jerking away. Instead he stared up to her—she would be taller than him until his next growth spurt—lower lip trembling with the chill that seemed to have affixed itself in his bones. If it was cold enough to make a dragon shiver, it was cold indeed, and the dampness didn't help.

"Not there," Maylin murmured, using her grip on his shoulder to turn him toward the west. "Try there."

Before Tylen, there was a strip of ice-rutted muddy field. What snow remained was stained with melted ash, running like poorly applied kohl makeup. In the distance, barely discernible, a dense forest reared up again from the barren winter landscape. The trees were dark and lonely sentinels in contrast to the fog and sky, and they thrust heavenward like bared wooden teeth.

The dragon couldn't help but think that it was probably beautiful to behold in the summer, but now... it was a good place for something sinister to hide; or a place for something wounded to go. Oh.

"Why are you helping me?" he finally asked Maylin, his expression calculating. He had been doing his best to escape her kindness for the last few days, and he was certain she had to be insulted by now—he would have been.

"Why aren't you running from me, dragonling?" She answered the question with a question, which gave him further pause.

"I'm not a child," Tylen grit out, assuming the direction of the conversation in the manner of one provoking in self-defense. Maylin reminded him of his mother, and everything that was simultaneously wrong and right with his flight. And like his mother, she was also a green dragon—which didn't help matters.

"No, but a young drake needs guidance. I may not have hatched you, but I am trying to look after you. That is, if you would let me."

"What do you want, then? Why would you bother!" Tylen's words were so suspicious that they even made him blink. He hadn't realized how deep his fear and pain ran; or, more aptly, he had been trying not to think at all.

"I don't want anything except for you to be safe and happy," Maylin replied gently, trying to de-escalate the situation.

"Then what do you want for your effort? Everyone wants something! Anyone who says they don't is lying."

"Get out of..? Tylen!" Maylin was finally starting to sound exasperated. "You're flight. You're a dragon, just like me. We've known enough hardship and loneliness. We are only as great as the love we put back into Anteas, and into each other. Is it manipulation to want peace and happiness for our people? If the world can hate without reason, can't I love without wanting anything in return?!"

Tylen stared at the other dragon. He had never seen her have an outburst, and that meant he was truly upsetting her—which he hated. The guilt twisted in his guts like a knife, but he couldn't push aside how much she unnerved him. He and his flight had never seen eye to eye.

Trying to take a step back from the conflict he had created while admitting he was out of line; he tried a different tactic. "No one wants me around. It isn't personal, but we must all look out for ourselves. You... you can't *care* about me, Maylin. You'll just get hurt." The words came out as sulky as the dragon himself, and he frowned down at the dirt. He knew he was acting infantile, but he couldn't seem to stop himself, either.

"It seems to me, that you don't want anyone to want you. Are you more afraid that you will be hurt, or that someone will hurt you? You and His Majesty have more in common than you know."

Her words visibly struck their mark, and Tylen tried to twist out from under her grasp. "Stop!" she snapped— her tone brooking no argument as the growl of her Draconic form bled through. "Look at me."

Tylen stayed frozen for a time, but he knew it was best to not argue with a female dragon when she commanded—so eventually he turned wide golden eyes to her. She had twisted her fingers into his robes to hold him fast, and every muscle in his body was tense as if he expected to be struck.

"When have you hunted and fed last? Did Copelan take you?"

"I... I haven't. I eat enough."

"Tylen, don't make me feed you like a stubborn hatchling!"

"I don't eat meat. I don't like to kill!" The words weren't an excuse so much as a protest, and they made the older dragon frown.

Maylin's hand let go of his robes and found its way up to Tylen's jaw, tipping his chin up so that their gazes met properly; he had relaxed visibly when she let go of him. "You're growing, and you need meat so that you can be strong. The next time Copelan goes, please go with him."

"I can't..." Tylen said thickly—his frustration resulting in a rush of gold-tinted tears that welled, but never fell.

"Tylen. You're a dragon. There is no shame in that. No one here will judge you for doing what comes naturally."

"But... what will Brynn think?" Tylen finally replied, voice wet with unshed tears. He was shocked at the words Maylin had plucked from him when he was determined to say nothing. His insecurities were frustratingly childish to him, and he already felt like he was losing the battle of perceived maturity.

"Oh, Tylen." Maylin found herself stroking both thumbs over the blond dragon's high cheekbones. She saw the tears in his eyes... and her sister in him in a way she hadn't with anyone else. "Tylen." Slipping an arm around his waist, she pulled his uncertain form against her, rubbing his back until he went submissively limp.

Resting his cheek against her shoulder, Tylen hid his face with a chirp of misery. The sound was Draconic—and as juvenile as it was soft—but Maylin heard it; and she smiled. "We're your flight now. All of us, even Grayden.

We're here for you. You don't have to do everything on your own. You, or Brynn."

Tylen didn't reply, but his hands fisted into the back of her robes, his trembling grasp having nothing to do with the chill.

"It will be alright," Maylin breathed, staring in the direction of Skyeford, which had finally been swallowed up in fog. "But you should go now. Your prince isn't far. I, on the other hand, have Lady Rose to retrieve."

Picking his way as delicately as he could through the mud, Tylen reverted to his Draconic senses—they were muted in his human disguise—and frowned. Maylin was right. Brynn was here. Even with rain and mud confusing every scent in the forest, he could tell. He simply hadn't been headed in the right direction before.

Unlike any human that Tylen had met, the dragon could feel Brynn like an exposed nerve. Happy or sad, tired or energetic, Tylen felt the change in mood like an elementalist knew the variations of their element to call... and the closer he drew to the other boy, the stronger the sensation became. It was akin to the feeling of pressure that accompanied arkane magic—and in the same way, it was mercurial.

Tylen didn't know what that meant yet, but perhaps it was something he could ask Grayden about if the opportunity presented. He suspected that despite the archmage's jocularity, if he reached out with a question like this, he wouldn't be laughed at. It was getting past his own pride that was the hard part.

Chapter Two

Brynn contemplated the crumpled form at his feet. Even if he closed his eyes, he still saw the scene before him—mud churned despair, splashed in the dull red-brown of old blood. From where he perched on an icy rock, death was all he could think about. If he was honest, he had been trying not to think at all. He was relieved that he hadn't found his father's corpse; but in a way, this was far worse—the proof in the details.

He had been following an unusual set of tracks as Ella had taught him, wondering if he had stumbled upon evidence of his father's escape. What he had found instead was a pregnant human woman. He suspected she had been separated from a family group escaping Skyeford—too heavy with child to keep up. The dead woman was curled onto her side in the mud, eyes staring straight ahead at what had been her last sunrise. She still appeared deceptively alive despite her less than recent death—cold preserved corpses startlingly well.

What had killed her hadn't been the coup and

subsequent route of her city; it had been some sort of predator. Her right leg had been severed at the hip by massive jaws, but she had no other visible injuries; so she must have managed to drive off her attacker. Knowing she was dying, she had dragged herself to the clearing to bleed out as the sun rose. Unfortunately, that wasn't the darkest part of the grisly picture. What had attacked her hadn't been a bear. The tooth marks left in naked, yellow hip bone were too big for that, and what it hinted at left the prince feeling cold inside and out.

Tucking a stiff tendril of brown hair back behind her ear—a last act of respect—Brynn then reverently brushed the curve of her swollen belly with an index finger. The wet fabric of her tunic stretched taut under the strain of her gravid form, and the sensory memories rushed back to him. It reminded him of the day his mother had died, and he paused, feeling nausea climbing up the back of his throat.

He had been too young to understand, then. He had only been seven. His mother had been older, thirty-six, and there had been concern about the health of a second pregnancy. He had other fears as a child, worrying that his mother and father wouldn't have time for him; and more than once in childish rage he had wished his unborn sibling dead. Then it had happened, and death had taken his mother, too. Logically, Brynn knew it hadn't been his fault, that he had been a child and hadn't really hated his brother. Still, death had come. And taken. And taken. So Brynn had resolved himself to live for the boy that had tasted only one breath before he faded. It had been the right thing to do...

"I'm sorry," he whispered to the dead woman, wet, wavy hair plastered to his forehead and neck. He had lowered the hood of his cloak out of respect, and he couldn't bring himself to put it back up. "I'm so sorry I failed you. I can't even bury you properly. I should have seen this coming. I should have known... I could have done something. I know I could have."

"No. You couldn't have."

The familiar voice made Brynn startle and pull his hand back from the corpse in surprise. His blue eyes were wide, and his teeth were grit when he whipped around to face Tylen.

The solemn look on the dragon's face took Brynn's breath; as did the hesitantly outstretched hand, fingertips tentatively reaching out to touch his shoulder. Tylen hadn't quite managed to complete the gesture, but his gold eyes were glowing with sympathy and unspoken emotion.

"How much of that did you hear?" Brynn asked.

"Does it matter?"

"I suppose not," Brynn murmured, staring down at the dead woman again. This time he didn't look through her, and he forced himself to really see her. The shape of her nose, eyes, and lips. A woman who had lived, and loved, and laughed before she met a grisly end. He deserved to be shown the truth of his failures.

"It's not your fault," Tylen said firmly.

"I am king. Yes it is. I failed her, and her baby."

"You didn't kill her, nor did you wish for her death." The dragon crouched in the mud, examining the body thoughtfully. "And it seems I am the one who should be sorry."

"Why, Tylen?"

"It was a dragon who did this," Tylen replied, brow furrowing as he silently sniffed the air.

"It is no surprise—there are dragons among the Separatist ranks."

"That's not it. That wasn't just 'any' dragon," Tylen said, voice breaking as he swallowed hard. "I recognize her scent."

"Who was it, then?" Brynn's eyes narrowed as he glanced down at the top of Tylen's bowed head, having trouble looking at the corpse again.

"My sister did this. This is my fault. She's here for me, and I should have stopped her. Prince... you must understand that you could not have prevented this."

"Is your sister that violent? And if she killed her,

why didn't she eat her?" Brynn looked deeply confused. They had discussed that Tylen had a living sister, but no more than that. The prince was doing mental math and not getting the sums he hoped for, knowing what he did of dragons. He'd heard the whispers about Separatists ties, and he wondered if the naysayers had been right about Tylen all along.

"Dragons don't eat humans," Tylen said sternly. "Not even Lukka, as crazy as she is. You all for... lack of a better explanation, taste terrible."

"I don't follow."

"I don't, either. But I feel like the answer should be right in front of me. All I know is that my sister wants something from me, and I am not giving it to her." Tylen stared down into the woman's glassy, unblinking eyes before glancing up to Brynn. The other boy looked away quickly so that Tylen didn't see the tears threatening. "I don't think she'd take a trophy, that's not how she works. Are there other cases of bodies missing parts?"

"There have been other bodies like this," Brynn nodded, then choked, covering his mouth with the back of his hand to swallow a sob. "Ears missing, hands missing for no reason... I don't understand. The Angelic invaded the city directly after the coup, then disappeared again with all manner of body parts. More than one survivor saw it; is

17

your sister working with them?" Brynn refused to believe Tylen was a Separatist. There had been ample opportunity for the dragon to kill or kidnap him, and he'd done no such thing. Grayden seemed to trust him, too; and if Grayden could trust a dragon, everyone could trust that dragon.

"Come back. Let's not think about it now," Tylen said with more certainty than he felt—shaking his head as if it could drive the specter of fear away from where it hovered between them. He rose stiffly, the cold making his healing leg ache. He didn't quite know what to do with human emotion, but he was trying.

"I can't." Brynn shuddered, teeth chattering.

"Yes, you can. You're human. It is cold and raining, and you will freeze to death eventually. On that note, when have you slept last? Or eaten?" The hypocrisy of his questions wasn't lost on the dragon, but he wasn't above shaming Brynn if the situation called for it. He also didn't want to think about Lukka anymore.

"It doesn't matter. All that I care about is that my people are dying, and I can't stop it!" Brynn's volume rose with each word until he was practically shouting, his temper breaking at last. It was fury that had him rising from the rock, his hands fisting into the front of Tylen's wet robes. Trembling, he gave the dragon a shake that made his teeth click. "Tell me what to do!" he demanded, tears joining the rain streaking down his face. "Tell me what to do, and I'll do it!" He choked on his words—the fight, and volume, going out of him as quickly as it had come. Then he whispered something so quietly that even a dragon's superior hearing couldn't catch the words.

Tylen's big, gentle hands clasped over Brynn's forearms—he still had a great deal of growing to do, but he was taller and stockier than the prince—and he frowned. Brynn's robes were soaked through to the skin. "You're drenched. You do no one any good dead of—what is that illness you humans are so prone to in the winter—pneumonia, is it?"

He had no idea what he was doing when he pulled Brynn closer, but the other boy didn't shy away when offered an embrace. He was lithe and sinewy in the dragon's arms, and as cold as Tylen suspected; technically borderline hypothermic, so warmth couldn't wait. "Come. Some rations, a hot drink, and some sleep would help us both. We must live to fight another day."

"I can't... I don't even know where to start!" Brynn lamented, hands kneading despairingly in Tylen's robes. He knew he shouldn't let himself be vulnerable like this, but it felt like he was falling apart, and he couldn't hold himself together anymore. Either his faith would be misplaced, and he would be dead, or Tylen would have some idea of how to make this better.

Tylen took a deep breath; savoring the feeling between them, and the unique scent and aura that made up Brynn as he knew him. When the dragon stepped back at last, knowing they had already lingered too long, he took the prince's bare hand in his gloved one—aware there could be consequence for touching the Crown. "Walk with me?"

"What of her?"

"We can do nothing, but I promise you this. I will avenge her. My sister is a problem I should have dealt with a long time ago."

"Your sister didn't do this by herself," Brynn said, his words as much a question as a statement, needing Tylen to fill in the blanks for him.

"No. Lukka did not. She much prefers to kill in her human form. As I said, humans taste terrible."

"You're not comforting me. Does she work for the Baron? For the Separatists?"

"There is no comfort to be found out here, or in the answer to that question, so come." This time, Tylen gave Brynn's hand a slightly more playful tug, sidestepping the seriousness of the moment. "We will sort out the mystery soon, of that I have no doubt. Grayden will help us find the answers we seek."

"You mean, he's going to squeeze the truth out of

Donovan?"

"Yes. Exactly that. Now come, let me fly you to Helith. It's a safer place for a prince to rest." There was nothing Tylen could do to make this better, but if there was one thing he had learned in that filthy brothel in Sine, it was that sometimes the truly horrible things had to be ignored for the sake of sanity. Especially when they were things that couldn't immediately be made right. They would be, though. He would find a way.

Grayden sat at the makeshift table, wishing that he could feel his feet. The slats of the supply crate he was hunched on creaked ominously every time he took a breath, and the rough surface of the ammunition barrel beneath his elbows was catching on the fabric of his robes. Thunder rumbled outside the cave mouth, and the patter of rain echoed inside and out; one of the nearby branches of the cavern was open to the elements—which was something the archmage had become intimately familiar with it over the last few weeks of sleeplessness and combat.

Across from him, Sarah was helping herself to a hot mug of tea. It had been served inside a polished deer skull cup because basic cooking utensils, mugs, and bowls were not to be had unless Skyeford was raided for them. A clove cigarette dangled limply from her fingertips, unlit. It was Grayden's last one, and he had opted to give it to her.

Lightning flashed as the wind picked up outside, swirling against cave walls and carrying with it the musk of desert sands, snow, and ozone. A trail of water that had been steadily working its way in from the entrance finally met the side of Sarah's boot. She stared down at it impassively for a time... then lifted her foot up. It wasn't comfortable like that, so she eventually shifted positions, choosing to hug her knees to her chest for warmth. "I don't like this," she said as Grayden reached over to light her cigarette. She only took a drag out of habit, and when she did there was concern etched on her face. She offered the cigarette over to him. He looked like he might refuse, but she proffered it a second time, and he finally took it from her.

Taking a deep lungful of pungent clove, the archmage held his breath as he offered it back again, letting the smoke slowly trickle out of his nose as he absorbed her words. "I won't be gone for long."

"Grayden, who do you think you're fooling? You don't plan on coming back. I know you. Whatever you do or don't do... the outcome will be the same. You are needed here, not throwing your life away out there." Her brown eyes were filled with tears, and her lips trembled as she took another drag—then choked on a sob laced with smoke.

Sarah was almost seventeen years younger than him, but she barely looked it anymore; especially when she was worn thin from the stress of war. It made Grayden feel guilty. She refused promotions to stay at his side, and he had never asked her to leave. That was just how it was between them. And she deserved better.

"I'm coming back. I have promises to keep." He sighed. "And I'll survive Ambis like I did every other sortie in Sine. I don't plan to go out unless I'm taking every Angel with me."

"I also don't trust *him*... rogues are nothing but a betrayal waiting to happen," Sarah said, glaring; shifting to the topic of greatest concern with little preamble. Her wet-eyed gaze traveled conspicuously to Donovan where he crouched by the entryway fire. Sarah didn't always share her thoughts or feelings directly with Grayden. She was more the sort to drop hints. But not today. She hadn't been herself since she'd held them all hostage with an arkane grenade—forcing Donovan to tell them everything he knew. Well, Grayden doubted 'everything'… but it had been a start.

The rogue turned to peer in Sarah's direction as if he physically felt her glower, while Grayden said nothing and played his part well—meeting Donovan's eyes and giving him a slow, threatening nod. At that, the man in question looked away furtively, unconsciously scooting closer to Ella who was poring over a map in the firelight.

When the rogue huddled closer to her, Ella moved away with a bad tempered sound of frustration, and Donovan looked even more unnerved. He couldn't seem to find an ally outside of Vix, and the archmage felt a sort of sympathy for that—not that he would ever express that thought.

Sarah raised her cup of deer-skull tea in a silent toast that made Donovan frown, and Grayden had to look away. He didn't like the rogue, but he didn't approve of bullying him, either. "Don't think for a moment that I haven't got plans beyond 'A' and 'B'. I think I'm on plan 'Zed' now, and I'm adding numbers to mix it up a little." Grayden looked as tired as Sarah was stressed, and he couldn't hide it from her, so he didn't try. She sniffled once more, then rewarded him with a wan smile before she took another drag.

Progress.

"Alright, so, as long as you promise to come back, and that you'll keep an eye on the turncoat over there, let me change the subject again. Have you seen the hatchlings?" Sarah finally gave the archmage a smile that met her eyes.

There was a proverbial glow around her that reminded Grayden of an excited aunt meeting their niece or nephew for the first time. "I have. She's a lucky queen. Are they still hatching?"

"Yes. Six so far and six to go."

"A good sized clutch, then. She's going to be a busy dragon." He had never seen Sarah struggle so hard with her mood. Mind, she was a lieutenant in a remnant army, from a city and government that had been shattered. Skyeford had been betrayed by Parliament at the worst possible hour, and every outcast was surviving through pure grit and determination.

The civilians of Skyeford, and the fragments of her military, were homeless and vulnerable in a world under invasion. Right now, it felt as if they had nothing but vengeance to sustain them. Focusing on something small and good like new life—that was a much needed reprieve. It was also a vital reminder that they still had a shot at building a better future, no matter how dire their current circumstance.

"That she is." Sarah's expression sobered, then. "Has Brynn seen them yet?"

"No. I'm hoping to speak to him before I head off to play adventurer in Ambis. During that time, he'll be leading on his own. Make sure he visits them, okay? It'll be good for his morale." Grayden recaptured the cigarette from her, took a draw, then passed it back again. His fingertips brushed hers, and he could feel her warmth. He was still half frozen from his last sortie—and the subsequent flight back to the Foothill caverns. The weather was vile, warming up or no. His robes had only just begun to dry, and he felt sticky as well as cold.

"I promise. And who knows? Maybe you'll find the time to take him to the Clutching Hall—I really think it should be you. But if you can't do it, I freely admit to wanting to see them again myself... it reminds me of what we're fighting for."

Her words catapulted Grayden back in time. When he had first taken Sarah Carlson under his wing, she had been nothing more than a refugee from Sine. She wasn't a mage, and she didn't have a home. She had been a twenty-four year old bartender from one of the brothels who had fed Skyeford whatever intel her patrons were willing to pass on. Her only military experience was that her father had been a soldier. She had helped smuggle enemy information to Lynn Broderick and the war effort, and after the liberation she'd had nowhere to go.

King Broderick himself had encouraged her to enlist, then placed her in Grayden's division... and the archmage had gratefully moved her up the ranks. She might have been a null—she had no ability with magic—but she was like a mother to his men, and she was nigh-on unflappable. He didn't know if he was more touched by her tears tonight, or saddened by them, but he had enough strength to sit with her and hold the weight of her hurt while she put her head back together.

"That's the stupidest idea I've ever heard!" Ella snapped at Donovan, fracturing the silence and causing every nearby head to turn.

The rogue looked flustered, and almost embarrassed. "What I'm saying is that we have to pack light. We can get what we need beneath the wall—trust me on that."

"And if we're wrong?! Have you ever moved with this many men? We have captives to rescue. We don't know what kind of shape they'll be in. What if we have to provide for them, too? Hell! What if we need to carry them?"

"We're taking dragons, aren't we?" Donovan snapped.

"They aren't beasts of burden, Rogue...."

Grayden shook his head. It was going to be a long, long trip to the Walled City, and he wasn't looking forward to it.

"I might be glad I'm not going with you now," Sarah said solemnly.

"That's the spirit," Grayden deadpanned, letting his head drop into his hands. He didn't think Ella had found a way to procure cigarettes for the trip; but hope sprung eternal.

Tylen breathed a sigh of relief as he took Brynn's hand and led him into the barracks. He had flown fast, the prince tucked tightly against his neck ridges, and they had made good time. No one had batted an eyelash at a golden dragon landing in the courtyard—though a few sentries had taken appropriate notice.

Peering up in his human form, Tylen regarded the stained-glass windows and architecture above him. The once-stately building had been the city of Helith's town hall. A few weeks ago it had been nothing more than a pile of dead bodies; but then the 5th had taken advantage of the vacancy, and now it was a haven. The city had been cleaned up and repurposed as barracks for what remained of Skyeford's wayward arkane forces; and there was always something to be done therein.

Once-career soldiers were not content with resting on their laurels, which meant the building was bustling at all hours, and teeming with highly trained men and women of every calling. The raids on the Separatists that occupied

Skyeford had further galvanized the 5th, and now the barracks served as a true fort.

Speaking of which, an assault team had recently returned, and the healers were tending the injured; thus, Brynn and Tylen managed to sneak in mostly unnoticed. The prince was keeping his head down and hood up—and Tylen understood why. The other boy's eyes were puffy from tears, and he doubted Brynn wished to speak with anyone.

That was the terrible price of being born to nobility—the burden of the illusion of calm and confidence. It had to be harder for Brynn than most, especially with all the uncertainty surrounding his father's fate. "This way," Tylen said, spotting High Commander Jensen making his way into the commons on the other side of the gathering hall. Giving Brynn's hand a reassuring squeeze, he guided the other boy into the quieter hallway that led to the chapel—and away from his responsibilities.

Brynn had staked out one of the old closets within the vestibule for personal quarters, and Tylen assumed the other boy would want to be there rather than be grilled by the commander about his absence. The dragon prayed he wasn't wrong, that he wasn't overstepping—and his concern only grew when Brynn's footfalls began to falter.

Pushing back the creaky door to the prince's room,

Tylen noted how difficult the latch had become. The building had recently been brought back into square by engineers with nothing better to do, and now all the doors and windows were being... troublesome. "What is it?" he asked.

The prince let go of his hand and walked past him as if in a trance, motions weak-kneed; and long after Tylen shut the door behind them, Brynn stood stock-still, hood up as he hovered in the middle of the room. It looked like he might say something at any moment, but he remained mute and motionless.

It was the first time that they had broken physical contact since Tylen had found Brynn, and the dragon regretted it. It seemed like it might have been the only thing mooring the other boy to reality.

When he still didn't receive a reply, Tylen slid the deadbolt home as he did a sweep of the room with arkane and Draconic senses. Nothing. They were alone. The only sound was the drip of water from Brynn's sodden cloak, and Tylen frowned. "Do you need help? You'll feel better once you're out of your wet clothing. Even a dry blanket is better than what you're wearing now..."

"I can't."

Brynn's reply was so flat it was alarming, and Tylen reined in his frustration. "What do you mean?" he wheedled, trying to coax the other boy to talk, and to move past whatever was bothering him.

"I can't."

"That doesn't help me. What 'can't' you do?" Tylen hoped he wasn't pressuring Brynn when he finally approached him, raised hands guiding the prince's hood until it folded down over the tops of his shoulders. Brynn's long wavy hair had pulled up tight into frizzy coils, most of it having escaped its tie. His pale skin was even paler than before—the freckles that he had inherited from his father stood out starkly—but the most concerning change in his appearance was the dark circles beneath his eyes. He looked like he hadn't slept in a week. "My Prince?"

Brynn shook his head again. He was freezing beneath the dragon's touch, but Tylen's clever fingers had already set to work unpinning sodden cloak. The garment fell to the floor with a heavy 'splat'.

"You'll feel better out of these. Come now." Tylen knew this was a time for action, but Brynn still hadn't said or done anything. His breathing had quickened, and there was a tremble to his hands where they fell limply at his sides; but other than, he wasn't reacting in any recognizable way. "Brynn?"

The dragon seldom directly addressed Brynn by his name, and the way that cultured voice wrapped itself around the syllables made the prince's heart speed. He had never let anyone see him before, not since he was small... what would Tylen think? Logically, Brynn knew he had to change his clothes, and that he could send Tylen away if he wanted privacy... but he didn't want him to go. He didn't want to be alone, and he was caught somewhere between fear, arousal, and the desperate need to avoid the silence he so craved.

Tylen didn't know if it was right or wrong, but as it began to thunder outside, and the rain redoubled its efforts on the roof above, he decided Brynn needed a metaphorical push. He just had to figure out how to best go about it.

Focusing on his scent, the beat of his heart, and the rush of heat flowing beneath his skin, the dragon processed what was unique to the other boy. When the prince's blue eyes finally flitted up to nervously meet Tylen's gold, there were ghosts there—dancing silvery gray beneath the surface in that otherwise open face—and Tylen finally understood in a way that transcended words.

Despite what had been done to him in the back room of a brothel in Sine, and his uncertainty and self-doubt, Tylen leaned in. Carding wet hair back from Brynn's forehead and cheeks, he tilted his head, lips parted—and their natural gravity took care of the rest. Tylen's heated mouth pressed lightly to Brynn's cool, rain-wet lips, and for a moment both of them froze. Then Brynn was exhaling in a rush, and Tylen was breathing him in as the prince's shaky hands clasped the shoulders of his robes. The other boy was clinging as if for dear life, lower body arching into Tylen's sinuously.

Neither of them had expected the burst of passion between them, and as Tylen deftly worked loose the ties of Brynn's robes, the prince wordlessly begged for more kisses.

That was something that Tylen wouldn't deny the other boy—and when warm, wet tongue flicked across the dragon's lips, he opened to the clumsy exploration.

Thankfully, the prince was a fast learner, and all awkwardness had faded by the time the dragon had coaxed the wet tunic up and over his head. The moment the passing of the fabric broke their kiss was when Tylen took the other boy in his arms, guiding them down to the edge of the bed...

Then stalled.

Brynn was straddling Tylen's waist, his knees leaving damp marks on the blankets beneath them. In the dragon's lap, the prince was bare from the waist up except for the bandages around his chest. Bandages...

Tylen's gold eyes were glowing with a combination of desire and concern when he halted. He knew what he was looking at, but he hadn't fully processed it. Brynn had gone still, noticeably holding his breath as he waited to see what the reaction would be; and without being told, Tylen knew he had to respond correctly, or he would break this thing between them forever. "Are you hurt?" he finally whispered, the claw-like tips of his fingernails tracing lightly over the wraps. The gesture was curious and worried, not betrayed.

Brynn shook his head. "Not hurt," he rasped, voice low with stymied desire... and fear.

Tylen could still feel the heat of the other boy against his belly, but there wasn't an answering hardness against his. Oh. "Are you..?"

Brynn didn't let him finish his sentence, already he was trying to scramble off and away—but Tylen caught him around the waist and followed him up when he stood. "Wait. Wait!"

Brynn felt the tears of shame start, and he couldn't stop them. They came without warning, and all he wanted to do was get away. Every time he tried to pull back, though, Tylen was in step with him.

"Wait," the dragon kept insisting, putting himself between the door and Brynn.

"Why? Please... please, gods, if you don't want this, please don't tell anyone. It's bad enough as it is."

"Brynn..."

"Please. I'll beg if I must—"

"—Brynn." Tylen was desperate to get through the other boy's panic. He hadn't let go of him yet, and slowly, carefully, he closed the distance between them again. "Take them off."

"What?"

"Take them off. They can dry with your clothes. You can wear my under robes until then. They're still perfectly dry. Mage clothing seems better suited for inclement weather."

Brynn was still trying to wrap his head around what was happening. He had been certain that Tylen would hate him, and he was still working through the motions of perceived rejection even though Tylen showed no sign of it. "You... have questions, I'm sure."

"They can wait, and only if you feel like answering them. You owe me nothing." Tylen was already letting his cloak fall to the floor and unzipping his outer robes. "Get warm, Brynn."

"Does this mean you won't say anything?" Brynn asked vulnerably.

Tylen shrugged the dry and body-warmed fabric of his under robe from his shoulders, letting go of Brynn only long enough that the other boy could turn away. As the prince's hands hesitantly worked free his chest bindings, the dragon draped his robes around Brynn's shoulders from behind, helping him to tie them as the wrapping fell away.

The dragon was careful to protect the prince's modesty, and he pressed his cheek to the other boy's shoulder blade to check himself. He was still very much aroused, but Brynn would let him look when he was ready. *If* he was ever ready. For now, Tylen considered the encounter over whether his libido liked it or not. "Better?"

Brynn took in a long, shuddering breath. "Better," he replied tearfully, stepping out of his soaked trousers. The robe covered him, and he was emboldened by the fact that Tylen hadn't run. Feeling some of his shivering ease, the prince snuggled deeper into the dragon-warmed fabric. It smelled like Tylen—hot arkana, wood smoke, and winter winds.

ukka strode across the polished marble floor, a sinister picture of grace and schooled disinterest. If the Baron didn't know better, he would have said that she didn't care about the precariousness of her position; but experience told him it was quite the opposite. The more avoidant the young dragon was, the more trouble she was in. She was only flirtatious when she thought she held the high ground. She also wasn't one for niceties, so he wasn't surprised when she launched immediately into her report.

"The Angelic moved in too quickly. Your son was meddling in affairs he had no business in, and he gave the Cideshii operatives a chance to warn the Archmage. Crushing Skyeford did nothing more than force Grayden's hand, and we cannot deny involvement for much longer. The ambush at Belden was far too bold a move, and we were watched. The evidence is stacked against us."

The young dragon had inclined her head when she paused before him, but she wasn't yielding. It wasn't in her nature to bend her knee, and he wouldn't ask her to. Not yet. The day would come when she would be on both before him, but it was not today.

He waited until she began to fidget, then leaned forward in his armchair. The book he had been reading was draped over the armrest, and the pages whispering against the sleeve of his suit was the only sound interrupting the ambiance. Distantly, thunder grumbled—the rolling as regular as a sleeping man's breath. It might have been peaceful otherwise. Instead, the tension grew. "All to plan, Little Queen. What do the victors care for the voice of the defeated?"

"Your arrogance will devour you! I know full well that one of the Armored survived and told all he knew. They *know* what we did in Belden, Forscyth! They know what we did in Skyeford. Parliament was instantly divided the moment you struck, and those that you believe you own are not as loyal as you think."

"They'll come around, Pet."

"You know of the cure. You think you can offer that to the Angelic? That they will get well, then crush those who have been withholding it from them for so long?"

"No. I'm going to give the dragons to them. They can do what they wish from there. Make a cure. Make charcuterie. In return, I believe our Angelic headaches will finally leave this planet. Maybe they will take the insects with them as slaves."

"And say that they do as you think? Say that our blood and some foul-smelling insect slaves are enough to satisfy them. Do you really believe that they will leave?"

"They will be grateful. They will run once they have what they want. Why stay here, where they are so ill-suited for the climate?"

"You think they will hand over the reins to you. Gods help us, you *actually* think that."

"I think that criticizing my performance is a poor decision on your part. I don't see a dead Archmage. I don't see the graves of Broderick and his whelp!"

"You don't have that much support, Baron. Not enough to be this bold. The only other option is to hunt down and slay the half of Parliament that remains loyal to King Broderick. Of course, I might be forgetting to mention that to do that, you would have to eliminate most of the mages. Then, of course, you would have to destroy magic altogether, and I don't believe even the gods can do that." Lukka's green eyes flashed as her temper rose.

"You are nothing more than a second-hatched spare. You're lucky I allow you to skulk about in my presence. You assume much, and know little. You will never be Empress. Your flight will never welcome you back, not after what you've done. Who I kill doesn't matter anymore—it all comes down to one thing. One. Thing, Lukka. One thing that you can give me that will spare your miserable, recreant life."

Lukka's hands clenched into fists until her claws broke the skin of her palms; sending drops of glowing Draconic blood to the floor along with the rainwater from her hair.

She knew better than to fight him. She was furious, and he had no doubt she would put her talons through his heart if given the chance; but there was no one she hadn't offered up on her deranged quest for power—herself included—and he could, and would, use that to keep her in check.

"Bring me the key, Lukka."

Lynn lifted his head from where he had been bowed over, hiding his face in Jasper's mane. His eyes were already sore from the fire, and now they were gritty with sand from the dust storm. He and his mount were lucky they had found shelter where they had—an empty Draconic temple. Then again, skill played a part in that, too—Lynn had remembered seeing the place marked on a map when he was a child; and with knowledge of desert geology he'd found it quickly enough.

Over the course of several days, horse and rider had alternated between trotting, galloping, and taking short naps in whatever shelter was available; and the weary king could hear as well as feel the animal's raspy gasps for breath. Dust storms could be deadly, and horses could die from blindness and pneumonia from exposure. To make matters worse, the salt that the storms picked up from the edge of the eastern salt flats could burn human and animal skin when wind driven. He wouldn't have risked traveling in such inclement weather if he hadn't feared pursuit more. It would be fine, though. He still had a few tricks up his sleeve—such as knowing the way the trade winds would drive the dust.

He had left his attackers behind and ridden the edge of the storm's downdrafts toward the Tel'av river, the blinding sands separating both parties as surely as a wall. The foothills of the Eastern Mountains tended to push sandstorms away into the ocean, breaking up the weather event; and their appearance on the horizon heralded the arrival of good drinking water.

The Tel'av river ran brackish closer to harbor, and he would need clean water for Jasper to drink. There had been no time to properly provision before having to flee— and water, as a horse would consume it, was in short supply. One might think that a desert had little drinkable water, especially when salt flats were involved; but southern Tel'aven was the true heart of the land, and it was nourished by the melting snows of the Eastern mountains. It was also home to the legendary white city of Tel'dorath.

Tel'dorath was once considered the capital city of continental Tel'aven. It surrounded a marble and limestone palace built in the center of a fresh-water lake. It was where the Flights held court, and the Draconic Emperor or Empress dwelt with their kin.

When the dragons had been part of Parliament, Lynn had visited the Draconic capitol. The palace had been impressive, and the dragons a sight to behold. They might have been culturally different from humanity, but their thirst for knowledge and their custodianship of lore was nothing short of heroic. Their thoughts on life and death were also very different. Due to their longevity, they viewed themselves as guardians, or stewards, and it was noble to say the least. They hadn't deserved what befell them, and even after they had abandoned their seat in Parliament, Lynn had lost no respect for them, or the empress that led them.

"Don't worry," he rasped as Jasper shook his head, snorting in protest at the way sound echoed within the temple. "We can rest here for a while. No one is going to sneak up on us with this." He gestured outside, as if the animal might understand him. Dismounting, Lynn swayed dizzily. He was still tired and weak. "We might as well look around, right? This could be an adventure." The optimism was for his benefit, not the horse, but he would fake it until he believed it if he had to.

Making his way unsteadily to Jasper's head, Lynn used the sleeves of his coat to wipe out nostrils and eyes, checking the horse over. The beast's long white whiskers contrasted with his roan face to make him appear surprised, but he seemed mostly undamaged. He was also starting to give Lynn 'the look,'—which was just glorified begging for apples, and a proclivity that had been discussed regularly within Skyeford Keep.

After taking a moment to steel himself, Lynn sighed theatrically. "I have no more apples, I'm sorry. I also know you won't like it in here." As a rule, horses didn't do well in caves. "And to be frank, I don't either. At least we have a place out of the wind, yes?" Jasper snorted again at that— still trying to clear his nostrils of sand—but let Lynn slip the reins over his head and lead him further into the long temple gallery.

It was dark and close, but the paintings within were radiant. If he'd had a torch, Lynn would have lit it to see the murals and glyphs better. He hadn't explored this area of the desert when he was a child, but he'd heard rumor of the place. He and his friends would have liked it… which meant his mother would have absolutely forbidden him to come here. He thought of her, and faltered for a step—in which his mount tried to walk up the back of his heels.

Jasper was as hot and tired as his rider, but every step he took was prancing; the echoing clop of his hooves making him jittery in the enclosed space. The sound was further manipulated by the roar of the wind outside, and the gusts howling around the underground pillars.

Indoor Draconic temples were rare, and it had been providence, or perhaps, fate, that had drawn Lynn here. When dragons died—usually after a long and illustrious life—they were buried at the heart of, or near, the place they loved. It was believed their spirits resided therein and continued to watch over the land and people they once tended. Many temples were open to the sky—a testament to Draconic love for the stars.

Closed temples were different. Closed temples tended to be places of learning and teaching. At their center there was a funeral casket that held the remains of a dragon who was gifted at their studies, and the temple would be built around it and dedicated to them. He suspected this was one such place.

The storm would rage for several more hours—days if they were unlucky—so there was time to explore. If Lynn was right, there would be a large secondary chamber within that had places where acolytes had slept. There might even be a deep indoor well that the dragons drank from, which Jasper would be as grateful for as Lynn.

"Well, friend," he began, looking back to his horse's nervously rotating ears. "I fear we aren't going to be able to meet anyone in the city. What do we do now?" Jasper bobbed his head in silent reply, and the king sighed again. "You're right. Everything's a mess, but we'll figure something out."

Lynn's thoughts had taken a gloomy turn despite their moment of good fortune. Normally he would have loved to explore such a mysterious place—but all he really wanted to do was hug his son, and spend a long night in Grayden's arms. That was, if the other man was still alive. The ghosts of the past were too close here, and they twisted the scars of grief around his heart until he could scarcely breathe. The familiar musk of desert sands made him think of his mother, and he wished now, more than ever, she was still with him to give him advice. He was finally home, but more alone than he had ever been before.

Tylen was curled up against Brynn's back, arms tangled around his waist. He had been careful not to touch the other boy's chest, or even vaguely look in that direction—which was fine, because there were many things about Brynn to be enamored with. It was sad to see the prince like this, and the dragon knew without being told that this was not characteristic. The other boy had barely been eating, and sleeping? Well, Tylen hadn't seen him so much as sit for more than five minutes at a time. Keeping busy didn't keep one distracted from their problems forever, and it seemed that was the case tonight.

The boy in question murmured indecipherably while shivering; and in response, the dragon pulled the heavy woolen camp blanket closer around them both. It was Grayden's, and the universal hope—the archmage's included—was that it would comfort Brynn on the nights he was alone. It might not have done exactly as intended, but if nothing else could be said for it, it was warm.

Tylen was currently shirtless, believing the raw heat of his body might help somehow. Once he had convinced Brynn it was safe to lie down, the other boy hadn't been sleeping so much as... staring. "What is it?" He broke the silence, accented voice soft. It was a loaded question, a broad one, because so many things were wrong. Still, the young mage asked, hoping to get some sort of response.

What he received was a silent, heaving sob that shook both their bodies.

Confused, Tylen nuzzled into the still-damp waves of Brynn's hair. The fractured, multi-faceted light of the stained glass window above brought out the red in the prince's natural tresses—then painted the blankets and walls around them in intricate, sparkling patterns. It made Brynn's tears shimmer like watered down ink; and Tylen still thought he was the most beautiful human he had ever laid eyes on, grieving or not.

"I miss my dad," Brynn finally whispered. "I can't do this on my own. I can't... I can't fix this. I want to fix it, but I can't, and I'm not strong enough. I never have been. This body... it's wrong. It's all wrong. He never made me feel bad about it, but I always knew I was a disappointment. I let him down, and he still loved me, and I don't know why..."

Tylen propped himself up higher on the pillow, watching Brynn's lips as he spoke, the way they trembled, the way blue eyes that had previously darkened with desire faded to stormy gray. Humans were fascinating... and heartbreaking. Brynn was hurt in a way Tylen didn't know how to help, but gods knew he wanted to. He wanted to give back the joy that had once been there—he hadn't known Brynn before his loss, but he believed in what had once been. He would say so, too, if given half a chance.

"Why are you not enough? What is so wrong with

your body? Brynn, I know you hurt, but it isn't because you did something wrong—or that there's something wrong with you. You're afraid, and… it probably seems like you're all alone." The dragon adjusted his position again, this time so that he could nuzzle closer. "Just yesterday I stood on the outskirts of your ruined city. The forest there was teeming with life, but I have never felt more abandoned in all my days. I wondered how that could be. Then I thought back on the things people have said to me over the last few months. I think I was feeling alone because I believed I wasn't good enough. But what was really happening was that I pushed everyone away before they could reject me. It was self-fulfilling." He didn't mention Maylin's council, but he wasn't ready to just yet. This wasn't about him. It was about relating to Brynn.

Brynn didn't answer at first, his breathing speeding and growing rougher. The sound of tears dripping from the tip of his nose to the floor beneath their cot was almost deafening to dragon's heightened senses. "I'm… I'm so sorry. I tried to take his place, to make it right, but I couldn't. I thought I could be enough for the both of us…" he murmured.

That made no sense to Tylen, and with the arm that wasn't beneath Brynn, the dragon reached up to cup his cheek, turning his head until their eyes could awkwardly meet. Did Brynn mean his father? It couldn't be. "Who did you lose?"

"My brother..." Brynn hiccupped so hard it shook them both.

"Your brother?" Well. "Can you explain? I'll listen."

Brynn seemed to think about that for a moment, Tylen's question filtering through the vying emotions that were drowning out rational thought. "I can try?"

The words were fragile, and Tylen winced. "Go ahead."

There was a long pause in which Brynn looked like he was weighing how much he wanted to share against what he was prepared to lose... then plowed ahead before he changed his mind.

"I was born in a girl's body... and that wasn't right because I was a boy. I couldn't pretend to be something I wasn't, and I told my mother when I was seven. It was the same year she found out she was pregnant with my brother. She never said a word against what I needed, and she and my father made the decision to raise me as a son. It was a hard year, and I was resentful—afraid that they wouldn't have time for me, and that the baby would get more attention than me—or, worse yet, that he would be born in the right body, and they would like him more because he was less troublesome."

Brynn paused for a few gasping breaths before speaking again, countenance growing sallow as he warred with his conscience. "Sometimes I wished for him to die. It makes me sick to think of how selfish that was, but I felt it all the same. Then, he did die. And my mother died with him. And everything was a mess…" Brynn couldn't look into Tylen's sad golden eyes anymore, so he rolled in the direction the dragon's hand was guiding him, and buried his face in his shoulder.

Tylen wasn't horrified by anything Brynn had disclosed to him, and his hands moved to rub the other boy's back, curling him closer as his lips pressed into his hair. This was the closest the dragon had come to wanting physical contact with a human—the more filial comfort Grayden had showed him the only example—so he still didn't know if this was the right thing to do, but he was trying. "Brynn. It means 'bear', doesn't it? In the old human tongue?"

"Father called me 'Little Bear'," Brynn replied raggedly, smiling grimly through his tears at the memory.

It made Tylen want to weep for the other boy, but he did his best to listen instead of relate. This still wasn't about him. "It is a good name. A strong name, for a strong man. You still feel strong to me—and that's coming from a dragon. Why do you think you aren't enough?"

There was a long pause. "I promised, when we put them in the ground, that I would live for all three of us. For my brother, for my mother, and for myself. I took the best parts, the pieces of what made them… them, and I wrapped them around myself like armor. I took my mother's laugh, and kept my habit of lurking in doorways—it was hers, first, but I didn't think she'd mind. My brother only took a few breaths before he died, but he smiled in such a way that we all knew he was at peace when he left us. So I borrowed that smile. Now… now I realize I'm only pieces of other people, my father included, and what if you realize that? What if my kingdom does? Right now they need a hero, a king... and to some I'm no more than a stupid little girl playing dress up in her father's clothes..."

Tylen winced, his eyes falling shut as he leaned in to press a gentle kiss to Brynn's mouth—a kiss that tasted of salt and sorrow, but spoke louder that the words he whispered against them. "If you had been hatched into a dragon's clutch, the choice would have been yours to make. We would have given you a new name, a name you made for yourself, and you would always be addressed as the drake you are—even if you didn't grow a beard, or have the matching parts. It seems to me, you're exactly who you are meant to be, even if you've sewn pieces into the tapestry of your life. Brynn, I would love you no matter what your gender. I love you; and I would bet the fortune I do not have that others feel the same way. You can't make decisions for them, or for me, and if your father has decided that you are the Crown Prince, and his son, who are you to doubt his judgment?" Tylen stroked his fingers through Brynn's wet hair, claw tips teasing out tangles. "Please?"

Brynn only cried harder, but he finally nodded. "I missed my potion, and I feel terrible. Everything feels so terrible and I hate… I hate what my body does. It feels so unnatural."

Tylen's eyes slit open at that, the realization dawning. Oh. Oh. That. It explained the change in skin scent at times, and he realized that there had been no healer to tend to the prince so… "No matter what your body does, or how it looks, Little Bear, you will always be a man. I want to be with you, and I am not afraid. Not of that. Maybe I'm scared that you will hate me, maybe that you will leave me, but gods, no, never because of that. You are a good prince, and you will be an excellent king. I would follow you to the ends of Anteas."

"Don't say that!" Brynn sobbed.

"In matters of the heart, I will never lie to you, Prince Broderick." Tylen had been in the same position with Grayden not long ago—he knew how it felt, to not be able to stop being petulant—so he didn't back down.

"Please don't love me, I'll fail you, I don't know how to... to do anything. You're the only one I've even kissed..."

"Then kiss me again."

"What?"

"I'm right here. You're the first I've kissed because I wanted to. I'll learn with you," the dragon promised.

"I can't..." Brynn was hiccupping, tears still streaming down his face—but then Tylen was swallowing his grief, warm mouth on his.

"You can," the dragon replied, lips brushing against the other boy's as he spoke—then kissed him until he surrendered, hands tangling into Tylen's hair. Chest to chest, hip to hip, it was a dragon who drove Brynn's tears away, marveling at how strong and beautiful humans could be. And when Brynn cried himself out—abandoning kisses for some much needed sleep in Tylen's arms—the dragon couldn't help shedding a few of his own.

He, too, had lost a brother, and he was bewildered by how much Brynn had made him remember. The words he had spoken to his prince, he might as well have said to himself. He wondered if there was an answer to some of life's mysteries in that observation, or a much smaller gap between their cultures than he had initially thought.

Perhaps dragons and humans… they really weren't that different.

"Someday, I'll tell you about Rayen," Tylen murmured.

"Mh'kay," Brynn hummed as he tumbled into dreams—and Tylen smiled sadly. Everyone was so tired, and in ways that sleep wouldn't mend.

"They don't trust you," Vix noted as Donovan crouched down beside the fire.

Flicking absently at the mud drying on his trousers legs, Donovan nodded. "You have a knack for stating the obvious. Besides, give me one reason why they should?" There was the faintest strain of hurt to his tone.

The rogue had been out in the rain, helping to carry in foraged supplies. It was cold, dark, and wet outside the caves—terrible weather for any activity, let alone hunting and gathering; but it had been necessary, the refuge was low on food. The hunters had returned exhausted, and some steps of preparing game had to be done outside the borders of camp. Anyone who had been free, and some who hadn't, had answered the call. Bellies had to be filled, Donovan's included.

"Your attitude might not be the best, but there's a lot

you've said that I can't disagree with. Maybe I wouldn't have said it as you did; but just because you're a rogue doesn't mean you don't care." Vix rubbed his close-cropped hair, blinking slowly in the low light before crouching down beside Donovan.

"They're right to fear me. To distrust me. I call only one woman 'master', and that's because she'd have me drawn and quartered if I didn't." The rogue gave Vix an empty grin and a wink.

Vix saw through the bravado, shook his head, then sat down with a sigh, soles of his boots close to the fire so that the leather would dry. "It's more than that. You could have left at any time. I know they think you're here because you want something. Do you?"

Donovan laughed; a short, sharp bark of sound that would have drawn attention had the room not been empty—all available hands were processing meat in the kitchens. "Of course I do! I'd even wager what I'm after, and what Doc is, is exactly what the Baron wants to get his hands on."

"And what's that?" Vix asked plainly. Every man wanted something, it wasn't personal, it was reality.

"The key."

Vix tilted his head. "The key to what? What sort of key?" The two questions tumbled over each other so rapidly they made the rogue blink.

"Ahh, now if I knew, that would help a lot. But I don't know what the key looks like, or what it unlocks; only that we need it, and that, theoretically, it's a Broderick who has it in their grubby little paws. It was a gift a long time ago, from the dragons to the Crown."

Vix blinked again. "Dragons... It's easy to forget that they were part of Parliament, but it wasn't that long ago, was it?"

"No. Not even for a human."

"So you're looking for a key... and what else?"

"That's it. My most recent trick, other than slowly seducing you, has been letting them bully me into leading them to the place we need to unlock. I have to see the lock to know what the key looks like. Doc went ahead with her little team. I don't know if they've made any progress, but I'm supposed to follow up with the cavalry."

"Begging your pardon?"

"Sine. The Walled City. You know, the city built on top of a city? There's something there that the Angels want really, really bad. It got locked up a long time ago. The Angelic crashed here looking for it, and have been trying to make do, but I don't think they can leave until it's found. They're probably toast without it, to be honest. If you've noticed, they haven't been looking particularly good lately."

In fact, Vix had. "Have you told Grayden?"

"Naturally, I have not."

"Then why are you telling me?!" Vix's eyes flashed golden before he regained his control. "Don't you think this is important? He was facing you down a week ago, and you didn't tell him then?!"

"I do think it's important... but it wasn't time. Now it is, and that's why I'm telling you. Also, if Doc asks? It wasn't me who squealed. Addendum: you asked me to tell you, so I did."

"Why would you trust m—and you absolutely have not!"

"Have not 'what'?"

"Seduced me!"

"I've not, then? But you'd be receptive?"

"You're impossible!"

"No, that would be you. You've spent your whole life 'believing' you're a human. Even I can't delude myself for that long."

The fight went out of Vix at that, his head bowing into his hands. He rubbed his thumbs at his temples, as if to rid himself of a headache. It was actually a way to hide from Donovan's gaze. The gunner felt raw. "So we need a key—that we don't know what it looks like—for a place that we don't know anything about, in a remote, hostile city we probably won't ever come back from, for something that the Angelic want, that we—surprise—don't know much, if anything, about."

"That's the size of it."

"You expect Grayden to hedge his bets on this sort of thing?"

"Nope. That's why I'm telling you."

"And you'd trust a dragon?"

"A Half-dragon," Donovan corrected. "So, you admit it?"

"If you'll stop mentioning it."

"When did you have a clue? Something about a lake? Inquiring minds *have* to know!" Donovan said coquettishly.

"Oh, yeah... that," Vix trailed off, looking away and making as if he would rise and leave. He was always thrown off balance when the rogue's mood shifted from serious to playful.

Donovan's hand snaked out and caught his wrist. "Sit. Stop running away. It's nothing to be ashamed of. They allow dragons in the military now... well, what's left of the military, I suppose."

The gunner gradually slumped back to the ground as Donovan's thumb began to rub at his wrist—finding himself strangely comforted. He should have run. But he couldn't. Not when the rogue was touching him like that. "You'd really want to hear about it?" He lifted his head, glancing shyly into Donovan's bright green eyes, admiring the tendrils of dark, wet hair where they stuck to his forehead.

"Oh yes, secrets are my specialty. Learning them without having to torture them out of someone? That's even better."

"I suspected you'd say something like that," Vix groaned.

"Don't act so surprised... Now, are you going to tell me, or not?" Fingertips slipping along his skin, the rogue gave Vix's broad hand a squeeze that was much more solemn than his cheerful front.

"Yeah," Vix replied, sounding breathless and anxious. "Yeah. I think maybe it's time." He wasn't sure why he trusted Donovan; perhaps it was because the rogue was so honestly dishonest. Or maybe, it was because he was the first to care enough to see beyond the disguise, and hadn't hated what he had found. Vix had never expected someone to be willing to offer him anything more than camaraderie, and the entire situation was new territory. He did know that he liked most of what Donovan offered him, and that life was too short—Draconic or not—to spend hiding away.

Chapter Four

ynn snapped awake; more sleep was been badly needed, and he hated to move... but something had woken him. Blinking around blearily in the low light of the temple, the first thing he noticed was that it had gone quiet. The storm hadn't lasted all that long, a dozen hours at most, and all was silent now except for Jasper's sleepy breathing and the occasional fall of sand from limestone ceiling to floor.

Pushing himself upright on the wicker bed he had commandeered, the king set his bare feet down on the limestone floor, toes wriggling at the gritty texture of sand on stone. The room had not been meant for a man and horse to inhabit them, but the duo had made it work well enough. It had once been the headmaster's chambers, and there was plenty of space.

Lynn's head might have been aching, but he couldn't help reflecting on all that had happened over the last week; specifically, everything that had happened outside the bazaar. The Angels were here, hunting him, and they had moved swiftly. Worse yet, it seemed they weren't against working with the local sellswords. Since his mother had passed, Skyeford's relationship with Tel'aven had been shaky, and Lynn admitted it was his own fault for letting their alliance languish. He should have done more. His aunt still ruled the city, and he should have asked her for help. It had been instinctive to run, though. He had wanted to protect her, to take his own troubles far from her door.

Taking a deep breath to drive away the uncertainty and fear, he rubbed the aching tops of his thighs. He hadn't been in the saddle this much in ages, and despite the terrible things he had been through—and being woefully out of shape—he found he missed it. He had let himself become so entrenched in responsibilities that he had forgotten to let himself... be.

Stilling his mind, he focused on his senses. What he could see, hear, smell, and touch. Experiencing such things meant he was still real, still alive and able to make a difference.

The temple held the lingering scent of arkana and dragon, and despite the time that must have elapsed since the place last housed residents, the camel hides on the bed were soft—the woven reeds that made up the mattress of the bed were supple, if slightly worn. This was real. The good and the bad.

Looking at the colorful murals dancing across the walls, Lynn tried to decipher why he was anxious. He certainly hadn't felt unsafe when he had first found the temple. He had been curious, yes, but not frightened. Perhaps it was life experience that had him jumping at shadows. He knew how ruthless the Angelic could be, and experience told him to not stop running—that discounting the fanaticism of his enemies would be a mistake. But he was mortal, and he had to sleep.

The last few day's blistering pace had put distance between himself and his enemies, so there was time enough to draw breath. To not leap from one panicked decision to the next. He and Jasper had some rations to fall back on, and they had found a fresh wellspring at the back of the temple—which meant water enough to last them.

There was a composed air to the well room's construction, and it spoke volumes about the careful hands that had crafted it. What had once been a rangy upwelling of aquifer water had been transformed to a stone-ringed bubbling pool. It even had areas beside it for bathing and washing clothes. Such places meant bathing wasn't a waste of fresh water, so Lynn had given himself a rudimentary scrubbing last night. It had felt heavenly.

Still nude from his impromptu spit bath, the monarch's increasing anxiety prompted him to cast around for his smalls—they weren't far, and were dangling from a wall hook that, at best guess, appeared to be for drying clothing. If garments were hung in the right place, the hot air from the desert rushed in from the mouth of the cave and worked as quickly as any arkane drier.

Conceding defeat to his restlessness, the big man reluctantly moved to dress himself. Most of the clothing he had fled in was suited for winter, not desert travel, so it had been good to let his skin breathe for a time. That, and the opportunity to wash the reek of fire from his hair had been a siren song. He hadn't done an excellent job, but a bar of yucca soap laced with sandalwood had been left by the well—dragons were notoriously cleanly in their human forms—and it had improved the king's situation. The sleep had been the best, though. Proper rest, on a proper bed was a luxury he had taken for granted of late.

Everything about the temple hinted at comfort amidst the wilderness and a chance to tend his wounds. So why was he uneasy? It was trousers Lynn located next. They were made of heavy leather and the cuffs were fur trimmed, but overall, they were one of the lighter pieces of his regalia. He pulled his thin under-tunic on after that. He could throw his cloak over everything; it might have been made of wool and wolf fur, but it would prevent the sun from blistering his already burned skin.

Feeling fidgety, Lynn kept looking over his shoulder as he stepped into his boots and adjusted his sword where it buckled to Jasper's saddle. Something was wrong. Something he couldn't explain.

After taking a borderline-urgent trip down to the spring to fill water skins, the monarch offered Jasper a nose bag full of feed to distract him as he tightened his girth—then promptly felt bad. The warhorse looked as haggard as Lynn felt. His winter coat was already slick with sweat, and patches were falling out in moth-eaten clumps; the beast had begun to shed in the warmer climate. Everything felt out of place and off kilter. Like them. Like Anteas. And that feeling only increased as the king waited for his mount to finish his meal.

"Time to move on, I think," Lynn said, voicing the words because it made the silence less oppressive. He was determined not to think about Grayden, Brynn, or his people. He had to survive, and so far, so good. How he was going to make it back to the city to meet with Grigor, though? That was less clear cut than survival, and he would have to figure something out later.

Miles looked down at Brynn where the boy had curled into Tylen's side. The dragon had opened one sleepy golden eye to observe him—and the commander suspected that the only reason he hadn't been blasted through the wall with arkane magic, was because Tylen was too comfortable to move. With measured gestures, Miles stroked the top of Brynn's head. Wet hair had dried, but the texture was as wild as his father's when it hadn't been properly tended. It spoke volumes, and the commander wished he could make this better for everyone involved, especially Brynn. He thought of the boy like a son; and even though he couldn't take the hurt for him, he would have if he could.

Admittedly, Miles wasn't surprised to see Tylen here. He was glad of it, even. It seemed that Lynn had chosen well. Tylen was young, too young, but he had been indispensable over the last few weeks. For being a dragon, he understood humans well enough to keep Brynn from imploding—and considering how closely the two were entangled, Miles also suspected Brynn's secret was out, which Tylen had probably accepted as readily as he did anything culturally diverse.

How someone so soft—a dragon no less—had ended up with the military was puzzling, and if Miles ever had a spare moment, he planned to ask Grayden about it. "A hot bath would do you both good, and a meal. Maylin has been busy in the kitchens." Miles nodded toward Brynn who was nuzzling sleepily into Tylen's chest.

The dragon cupped the back of the other boy's head protectively, but he didn't push Miles' touch away, either.

"He hasn't been eating enough, and I'm glad you've gotten him to rest. The grief is gnawing at him like a sickness," The commander admitted.

"Is rest what he needs?" Tylen asked, the words vaguely defensive... but he was making every attempt to let Miles help. It was hard for him, but he was. "A bath, and food?" If he realized how ironic his statement about eating and self-care was, he gave no sign of it.

"Yes." Miles nodded. Dragons tended to be broody and overprotective, but only out of concern... which might have been endearing, not that the commander would say so aloud. Tylen looked so simultaneously lost and hopeful that it was hard to resist patting his head like a puppy. Love— especially love between two different species—was always a wild ride. At least Tylen and Brynn seemed to be good for one another. He had never seen Brynn light up the way he did around Tylen, and he hoped the trend continued. "This is an excellent start. A hot bath, a good meal, sleep, and meaningful touch are all excellent ways to help a human; no matter how they are wounded," he continued after a long pause.

"He isn't hurt," Tylen said protectively, the hint of a growl in his voice.

"Not physically, no, but humans can take wounds here..." Miles pointed to his own heart. "And here," he tapped his temple.

"So he *is* wounded?"

"Of course he is. But now that you are here, I think he can begin to heal."

"Do you really believe that?"

There was worry in Tylen's wide eyes, and Miles once again had to fight back a laugh. "I really do." Standing abruptly, the commander gave Tylen's blanketed leg a pat. "Once he wakes, why don't the two of you make use of the hot spring the Elementalists have created out back? I hear it's an excellent place to spend some time."

Grigor's sanity was hanging by a thread. He had lost track of how long they had been beneath the Walled City—and if he didn't taste fresh air again soon, he was going to start screaming and be unable to stop. Sevaren was faring worse. Dragons were not meant for such tightly enclosed spaces, and the elementalist was suffering as badly, if not more so, than the rest of them. A city buried beneath a city was both fascinating and frightening, and was, lightly put, narrow in many places.

"According to my charts, this should be the spot,"

Loux carefully unrolled the piece of parchment in her hand, holding it up to the faint light filtering in through an overhead city grate... which was several stories above them.

"You said that about the last place," Grigor snapped, then checked himself. Taking temper with Loux wouldn't make anything better.

Sevaren growled at Grigor before burying his face in Loux's back again. The dragon had been sticking close to her, touching her nearly constantly for reassurance. If Loux minded that a shaking, sweat-soaked, and claustrophobic elementalist was clinging to her—she had never said a word. Then again, when the group took turns resting, she would sleep in Sevaren's arms, stroking his hair until he drifted off. The two seemed to lean on each other, though Grigor had no idea if they were a couple. They certainly had an odd dynamic, but when it was the sort that worked, who cared?

The first two nights beneath the city, Sevaren had awoken screaming—and more than once nearly gotten them caught. There was a guard that walked the streets *beneath* the streets, and their purpose was to catch trespassers, especially people from outside the wall. Thus, Sevaren snuggling up with Loux had kept everyone safer.

Unfortunately, it looked like the dragon's anxiety was worsening again; this time in an area where the ceiling was high. The group's sanity was being sorely tried, and Grigor prayed they would make it through this. "Tell me again why we can't just go home now?" the healer asked rhetorically, crouching on the filthy floor. He was getting used to the stench of human waste and mildew that seemed to permeate everything below Ambis' street level.

"You know damned well," Chell snapped, her words grit out through clenched teeth. She didn't want to be here either, but the wages of their failure were bigger than their current discomfort.

"It's here. I know it's here," Loux said. "I can feel it."

"What I want to know," Sevaren rasped, pressing his forehead to the back of Loux's shoulder. "Is why the cure for Angelic mange is worth all this. Why is it such a big deal?"

"Let me be so bold as to answer your question with a question? I'm a doctor, and this is what we do." Chell clasped the dragon's bicep reassuringly, then peered upward. There were symbols painted on the ceiling above them, the colors still as bright as when the workmen had put them there during the time of the old world. Some things could not be dimmed by human filth and age. "Why do you think that this city was walled off? You're a dragon, your people have a long memory; so you tell me."

Sevaren looked to her dully. "The Crisis. It was after the Crisis."

"Yes, that's right," Loux said vacantly. "So many echoes down here. So much time, and so many people living and dying. It's all tangled up."

"And what happened during 'the Crisis', Sevaren? Not many humans know what that was. Too many of us died, and those of us with any knowledge of the old world holed up here, within Ambis."

"There was a plague," Sevaren answered numbly. "There was a plague, and a lot of humans died. There were few survivors, but those that did... they were immune. Most of the survivors wanted to start a new life, to rise out of the ashes. But some were fearful there would be another plague, and to keep anyone who might not be immune out... they built Ambis. And they live here. I don't know how they survive. They've turned a lot of the existing city into gardens, and they have a cistern that's the size of a lake near the old plant."

"The power plant," Chell explained to Grigor's look of confusion. "Once this world was powered by something called electricity and fossil fuels—not the arkane. The plant used nuclear reaction to generate power, which drove everything—from horseless vehicles to boxes that kept food cold. Everything that runs down here? That runs on hydroelectricity. There is an enormous dam not far from here, and the energy it still collects works reliably in the tunnels."

Grigor blinked at that, shaking his head to clear it before he repeated. "So we are looking for whatever medicine the survivors took to be immune. Why? Aren't you and I immune?"

"The Angelic aren't," Loux said dully, expression far away as her fingertips trailed the wall. "They came here looking for a cure. They won't leave until we give it to them."

"But what the hell *is* the cure? And what was the plague, for that matter?" Grigor looked ready to lose his temper again.

"I don't know," Chell replied. "But I do know that the answer is down here somewhere, and we are close. Our dear bug friend Drishk paid for that map with his life—the very map he snuck out of the Baron's home and into Grigor's hands." She pointed to the parchment Loux held. "We can't give up now. Once we find the door, we'll know what else we need."

"And then?" Grigor asked breathlessly.

"And then? I have contingency plans 'a' through 'fuck-my-life' to consider," Chell replied grimly, wiping her curly hair back off her forehead—leaving a streak of grime on her otherwise pale skin.

"I'm going to have to remember that one," Grigor said, admiring the rogue's sense of humor given their situation. If they survived this... Sevaren wasn't the only one who was going to have nightmares. That was, assuming the Guardians didn't catch them.

Vix found himself curled up behind Donovan, both arms around the rogue's waist, face pressed into the nape of his neck. The sellsword's hair had grown long enough that it was curling at the tips, and the gunner found it comforting to nuzzle into. He was unwinding slowly, and the longer he lay there the easier it became to find the right words.

The two had found a private corner of the cave system where it was quieter... not far off the Great Hall, but near enough to still have light from the fire. They had needed the seclusion. Vix was nervous enough about his heritage without a dozen dragons sleeping on top of them while he tried to compose his thoughts.

"I was by myself. I took the night off because I had some shore leave. I went for a long walk. It always felt good to be away from everyone else. I loved Kris like a brother, but I didn't always want to be on top of him in a tank turret. There was a big lake south of the Academy. The water there is cold no matter the season, and I liked to go swimming there."

"You're allowed to, you know?" Donovan said, feeling fingertips pressing up under the hem of his tunic, seeking the comfort of skin on skin. Some men needed that sort of intimacy when they talked, and far be it from the rogue to complain; though he might have been hoping that Vix would understand the full extent of what he was asking—and if the dragon was willing, so was he.

"To what?"

Well, there went that plan. "You're allowed to touch me, you don't have to be so hesitant, and you're allowed to go places and do things you like. You're not a slave, Vix."

Vix's hands froze where they had been stroking the curves of Donovan's lean stomach. "You have no idea, do you?" Those words trembled, and they were as vulnerable as Vix himself. The soldier was already on the verge of fleeing—he wasn't used to trusting anyone, let alone talking about how he felt. He was a stranger to his emotions, he always had been, and the strain of the last few weeks was catching up. "You have no idea what that brand on my shoulder means, or what it was like. I was very much a slave, and still am in my head. I don't know if I'll ever be free."

There was a long moment of silence, but Donovan's hand clasped tightly over Vix's; refusing to let the other man run before they had worked their way through what was happening. "You're right. I *don't* know. Feeling this way... it's why you keep moving, isn't it? You were on a leash, but you were always stretching it as tight as it could go. It must be scary to not have it strangling you anymore. It was all you knew."

"I don't know what to do," Vix admitted, each word aching, not accepting or denying Donovan's assessment.

"You don't have to fight me, and I won't ask you to trust me," the rogue promised.

"You shouldn't trust me, either. You have no idea what I can become."

"You think that. But I've seen a few dragons in my day, and I have one in my bed right now. Don't kid yourself. I know what I'm doing. I'm an idiot, but I'm aware."

"Rogue... Donovan, when I become what I... am, I don't have any control. I can only remember bits and pieces."

"Maybe you think that makes you a monster, but maybe you were scared. I doubt you lose your mind automatically. I've heard a lot of tripe about Half-dragons, but I don't think I've ever heard that one."

"I lost control, Donovan. I lost control and I hurt people."

"You're not a monster. Why don't you try talking to Maylin or Copelan? They seem to have this whole dragon business down, and I don't think either of them get preachy."

"I could never..."

"Well, if you don't want to hurt anyone, it's probably a good time to be proactive. You know how mages are. If someone doesn't give them some guidance when they're young and coming into their abilities, they can be... destructive. But their powers aren't inherently good or evil. It's the intent behind them. Something tells me you know that, but you've been too scared to challenge your preconceived notions.

"Dragons don't like Half-dragons... they think we're abominations."

"I don't think this is a good time for dragons to judge other dragons. I think we all have to get along or we're fucked. Just my opinion, mind, but at this point... you could probably be pretty helpful, what, with all those abilities of yours."

"I got attacked by an Angel."

"Oh, is that all?"

"I ate him."

"And?"

"It was disgusting."

"And?"

"I was scared to death."

"Sounds pretty normal to me, honestly."

"I only remember it in bits and pieces."

"It's probably better that way."

"Yeah?"

"Yeah."

"What have you been waiting up for?" Maylin asked, her hand over Grayden's. She had just returned with Rose, and the flight had been less than ideal. They had made it back in one piece, though.

"Mainly, for Brynn to get his behind back up here, we have work to do before I leave. I want to make sure he's prepared as best he can be. I promised to be by his side through this." Grayden was hunched next to the arkane heater in the Officer's Quarters of the Foothill Caves, back against the wall, knees pulled up to his chest. His hands were the only thing sticking out from under the blanket he huddled beneath, and he looked down to where the dragon's pale fingers contrasted with his olive skin.

"I'm worried about you going, Archmage." Maylin's

eyes were brimming with unshed tears. "You and Brynn are all we have left."

"I promised Sarah the same thing I'm about to promise you. It's not my time yet. I'm not going to die unless I have it on good authority I'll take out every Angel on Anteas at the same time; it can be a nice little trip to hell together. Until then? I refuse. Simple as that."

Maylin didn't look convinced, nor did she seem dissuaded. "Is that what you've been looking for? Death?"

Grayden sighed and reached for another blanket. He wanted to go back to sleep, not have this discussion—which lead him to consider how lucky he was that Maylin didn't think like a human. If dragons ever really knew what they knew, they'd be even more dangerous. "You really want to know?"

"I know you. Brynn knows you, and he's commented on it as well. You're not only out there for revenge. What are you doing? There's a pattern, I just can't see it yet."

"You're right. I suppose you want me to save you from hours of painful contemplation. Fair enough." Grayden held open the blanket to the dragon, and when she curled up into it against his side, he closed it again. The gesture was playful, but it was also respectful. Maylin had always been sensitive, even for a dragon. He didn't want her to start crying. He was deeply uncomfortable around tears, his own, and everyone else's.

Normally, Copelan would have been here to comfort his mate; but the big drake was currently flying down to Helith to pick up Brynn and Tylen—and it was a long, wet, turbulent trip with the current weather. Thus, Maylin was here, doing damage control where she could. He couldn't blame her, it was better than worrying about something that couldn't be changed.

"You'll really tell me, and you promise to not make a joke or change the subject?" Maylin was studying him like a bug on a pin.

"Now, when have I ever done something like that?" Grayden teased. She glowered. He sighed.

"Tell me."

"Alright, alright. Fine. I'm looking for clues."

"Clues?"

"I'm very certain that Lynn isn't dead. Like Brynn, I'm looking for clues as to where he might have gone. Also, if Grigor is still alive, I know he has the information I need, including information about Lynn. Since we don't currently have a Grigor in our possession, I need to fix that. I also need a better lock on where the rogue queen took our young master Forscyth. Getting Donovan to elaborate is like finding hen's teeth to pull them."

"It's more than that. The skirmishes, and the running yourself ragged..."

"I've been extracting confessions."

"What?"

"I need proof. We have it, now. Reliable proof that Baron Forscyth has betrayed everyone, including the Angelic. We need Parliament back and on our side. Half of them are still loyal to Lynn, and those on the fence will come around once we can get them all together in one room. The problem is, they're too scared to reconvene."

"Who remains for certain?" Maylin asked, snuggling closer and closing her eyes.

"East Harbor, Sine, and Xastin."

"And who have we lost?"

"Gent. Belden. Half of Cideshaa, and possibly Tel'strathos. Tel'dorath has had an empty seat since Brynn was a child. The Academy is in an uproar, and loyalties there are split right down the middle."

"Damn."

"I can fix it. We. Can fix it. We have Vix and Rose. We can have Lynn and Grigor. Brynn saw enough to testify; and him or not, Donovan knows enough for all of us. The rogue queen wouldn't be a bad hand to play, either. The bugs... we have a few on our side pulling for us. If we can get Parliament to convene and hold trial before it's too late..." Grayden trailed off sleepily.

"...You could always blackmail Parliament," Maylin said.

"I'm shocked, but I'm also proud. Care to elaborate?" Grayden blinked in surprise, not liking being forced to re-evaluate the dragon rubbing her cheek lovingly against the top of his shoulder.

"Don't you still have the assassination order for King Broderick's father?"

"In the Baron's handwriting. Arrogant bastard even put his house seal on it."

"He really thinks he's above reproach, doesn't he?"

"Among other things... yes." Grayden rasped.

"Can I eat him?" Maylin's tone was chillingly calm.

"Would you really want the indigestion?"

"It would be worth it."

"No it wouldn't. Now get some sleep."

Grayden shifted his position so that Maylin could rest more fully against his chest, the heater working well enough for now. Between her Draconic metabolism and the wonders of modern magic, he was hoping to not feel completely arthritic when he woke.

"Do you think Copelan is safe?"

"I do. He's a grown drake and he can handle himself in bad weather, just as you did. Go to sleep. He'll be back before dawn and you can greet him when he arrives. He'll want to catch a few hours with his mate, that's for certain."

"If you're sure..." Maylin's eyelids were heavy, and despite her intentions to be a shoulder for Grayden, she was already dozing off, a contented purr rattling in her chest. The flight to retrieve Rose had exhausted her more than she wanted to admit.

"I'm certain," Grayden replied warmly, amused at her narcolepsy. He wasn't going to be sleepless for much longer, either. Not if she kept purring. The behavior was something he had only recently experienced with Tylen, and it was more soothing than he had given it credit for. "How is Rose?" he tested to see if she was really asleep.

When he got no reply, he shook his head fondly.

ose paused, her fingertips lightly trailing down the cave wall. Staring into the area of the caverns that had been converted to a kitchen, she saw Sarah Carlson hunched over a makeshift table, a plate of food in front of her that she hadn't touched. Her eyes were closed in what looked like prayer... or suffering.

The room was completely empty except for some flickering arkane lanterns, the hearth fire already nothing more than a bed of embers. Those who were out on patrol or raids had already departed, or had returned and were sleeping. Last Rose had observed, Grayden was curled up with Maylin, and the only sign of life in the caverns had been a few dragons playing a chess with an improvised chess set in the Great Hall.

The Hall was spacious and easy enough to light with arkane lanterns, thus had become a place of relaxation for Skyeford's refugees and remaining military. It was a place she wouldn't have minded being. Instead, she was here, seeking out Sarah, and wondering what she was doing while knowing full well. Giving herself a mental shake, she finally stepped into the kitchens, adjusting her shawl over her still-wet robes. Tip-toeing past the lieutenant, she put herself to work stoking the fire again.

It wasn't the returning brightness of the flame that eventually roused Sarah, but the clink of poker on stone. The woman in question inhaled sharply, brown eyes disoriented as she looked around furtively—then turned to see what Rose was doing.

"Sorry to wake you," the healer said, putting the poker down and rising slowly, one hand clasping her elbow as she looked at the soldier. She knew better than to rouse a man with something in her hand that could be construed as a weapon. These were dark times.

"No harm done, I was dreaming… of a place I haven't been in a long time."

"A bad dream?" Rose inquired shyly, twisting some water out of her skirt before toeing her wet boots off by the fire. Barefoot, she wriggled her toes. She could feel Sarah's eyes on her, and the intensity was intimidating, so she didn't look up.

"Not… necessarily. Home wasn't always bad; it's just been so long since I thought about it." Sarah raised her arms over her head and stretched before she turned to look at Rose. "I see you've returned. Grayden's been worried."

"And you were in here worrying over Grayden, weren't you?"

"Do I do anything else?" Sarah asked, laughing tiredly before staring down at her unfinished plate. "I should warm this back up. I was so sleepy..."

"Let me do that," Rose said, reaching out to take the plate at the same time Sarah lifted it up. Their fingertips brushed, and Rose felt a warm fluttering sensation deep in her stomach. "Sorry," she said, blushing. Still, she took the plate, and crouching down next to the fire she nudged the tin into the embers to warm through.

"You're soaked," Sarah said, "Grayden wouldn't tell me where you've been. What were you doing?"

"Scouting," Rose replied, glancing up from the warming plate to meet Sarah's concerned gaze. The lieutenant's eyes were always so piercing, and when they were focused on her it twisted her up in knots. The attention wasn't unwelcome, just... intimidating.

"Where?"

"Gent."

"That's dangerous. If your father catches you..."

"It's a small price to pay. I know all the back alleys and hidden passages. It's my home. I know he will kill me if he sees me, but there were some things I needed to find out."

Sarah slid from her chair to come kneel beside Rose, the motion graceful and cautious. Lightly, she reached out to touch a strand of the healer's messy hair, tucking it back behind her ear. "I understand. Dry off." Reaching for a dish towel beside the buckets that served as utility sinks, Sarah pressed the dry fabric into Rose's trembling hands.

Rose could feel her blush worsening as she took the towel. Mechanically, she blotted at her face, and then her hair. Sarah was still watching her. Less intensely, but that was more for her comfort than anything else, and Rose knew it. "When you dream about home... about what it used to be like... can you remember anything good?" she asked. "Just now, when I was back in Gent, everyone looked like zombies. They're terrified. The whole city knows that Father is the one that ordered the destruction of Skyeford. Most think King Broderick is dead, and he was the only buffer against my father's rage. People are on tenterhooks trying not to draw attention to themselves. It's like this in Belden, it's like this in East Harbor. I hear whispering about the Crisis everywhere. I saw an Angel walking right down the middle of the street by the healing halls, and no one even looked up or tried to run. Anyone who gets sick with anything at all ends up burned alive outside of town. They shut down the hall, and I don't know where the Guild Master is... Sarah." Rose reached out to the soldier with a shaking hand. "What am I supposed to do?"

Sarah's eyes narrowed, her face sober as she reached back and clasped the healer's trembling hand in both of hers—which were steadier and much warmer. "I want you to believe in Grayden. He made a promise to me, and he's going to keep it. I'll make sure of it. I want you to believe that no matter what happens in Anteas, the sun will rise as it always does. And never. Never forget that love still exists. I know it's hard, when everything is so ugly and frightening."

Rose took gulping breaths to slow her heart, and to fight back the tears stinging behind her eyelids. Sarah's brown eyes were so soulful and calming that she was lost in them, and for a time she forgot how cold and tired she was. "Are you afraid?" The words were small and fragile from her lips.

"Terrified. But we can still find a way to fix this. We can put all this right. And someday? Rose... we will put a stop to the corruption and make our world safe again. People deserve to live out their lives in peace."

"You really think we can do that, after all this fighting and death?"

"I'd bet my life on it. Because there isn't any

alternative that I can bear to imagine."

The smell of burning bread drew Rose's attention away from Sarah and back to the fire; and abruptly letting go of the other woman's hand, she impulsively reached for the smoldering plate. The tin was hot enough that she dropped it on the mantle, pulling her fingertips back to her mouth with a sharp intake of breath. "Damn. Damnit! Why am I so stupid?" she ground out between grit teeth, flustered in a way she almost never was.

That only worsened when Sarah reached out again, taking her hurt hand into hers, kissing the backs of her knuckles where the skin wasn't reddened. "I have an old desert remedy for things like this," she said, making Rose blush further.

"You do, do you?"

"I do. But you'll have to follow me. My bag is back in the Officer's Quarters." She looked down. "And don't forget your boots. The dragonlings like to chew on them."

The wind had died out completely with the dust storm's passing, and the air had become stagnant with the promise of coming rain. Lynn was torn between putting his hood down so that it felt like he could breathe, or keeping it up to ward off the punishing sun. Steam rose from the surface of the Tel'av river, and already the reins were leaving sweat marks on Jasper's neck.

The sleep that horse and rider had scraped up had done some good, but Lynn still felt bone weary. Most of that was grief and the weight of his perceived failures—which were the sort of things that rest didn't fix—but physically, the king had also been through the wringer, and he was trying to treat himself with the same mercy he extended to others. That wasn't something that came easily to him, though.

More positively, he was home again. He knew the bellow of bull crocodiles and the roar of hippopotamus like his own heartbeat. The rasping of grasshoppers tangled with the clinking of bells—the local goatherds bringing their stock down to drink at the river's edge—and it was like a song.

Skyeford might have been his inheritance, but he had never cared for the snow. The frozen wilds and sprawling stonework of the city had been beautiful, but it wasn't really home as much as a promise kept. He patted Jasper's neck absently, drawing a pleased snort from the warhorse.

He remembered the first time he had experienced the wilds of Tel'aven, and it had been a stretch of river like this. He had been so small that his mother was still holding his hand everywhere they went. She had showed him how to judge if the river was safe to approach before leading him down to pluck a lotus from the water's edge. She had let him smell the fragrant flower before tucking it back behind her ear, and the scent was etched indelibly in his mind. It was something that always reminded him of her. Aya.

Her name had meant 'miracle', and had been the first words he had tasted from a language he had only ever equated to the color of his skin. During his first visit to Tel'aven, the part of him that had been cold and closed had opened, blooming like desert flowers after the rain. His father had imparted the knowledge of sacrifice, duty, and honor; but his mother? She had given him the gift of wonder, and to hear the voice of the land as her people had—was twice as valuable of a birthright.

She had been notoriously open minded, Aya, and her heart had been as vast as the oceans of Anteas. His father could never deny her anything—not that she had asked for much. She was the sort of woman who had been content with the miracles that happened every day. The small, good things.

She had taught an impulsive and impatient Lynn how to be mindful; how to slow down enough to see that the steps of the journey were the point. Sometimes Lynn lost sight of that lesson, but never for long. Neither Amelia nor Brynn would let him. Aya, the miracle—Skyeford's queen and Tel'aven's princess—might have died from the grief of her husband's murder, but her legacy lived on in her grandson.

Lynn thought of Brynn and smiled to himself. He was so like his grandmother. He regretted that the woman hadn't lived long enough to meet him. At that point in Lynn's life, though, the boy hadn't even been dreamed of. Lynn had been a young, terrified king who didn't have the time to entertain the idea of a wife, let alone a future. He had recently buried his assassinated father, and had watched his mother die of a broken heart. Times had been dire; but like all bad times, they also hadn't lasted forever—just like Anteas' current predicament wouldn't. The world moved forever onward.

Gaze turning toward the river again, Lynn halted Jasper on a flat, jutting chunk of limestone. Dhows scooted up and down the waterway; and those going upstream ran near-silently on arkane engines. The violet glow beneath the water was the only thing that gave away the technology—that, and the crocodiles who chased the flashing lights.

When Lynn had been a boy, those boats had noisy motors that stank and ran on rare fossil fuels from the old world. But there had been little of that fuel left, and soon, much cleaner arkane technology had replaced it—mainly because the earth had nothing more to offer. The Crisis had changed everything about human ways of life. Lynn might have been a child at the time the last vestiges of old world technology died out, but he still remembered it faintly. So much was different, even for the grandchildren of the first generation.

Shooing the gnats away from his eyes, the irritable stomp of Jasper's back foot rocked Lynn in the saddle. It was beautiful to stay and watch the water, but they couldn't stop for very long. With the approach of the rains, the insects grew fierce, and Lynn was already sore enough with healing burns—he didn't need bug bites on top of them.

"Come on, then," he said, needing to speak, and to ground himself. Jasper snorted to him in reply, and that was sufficient acknowledgment—or at least, it was enough to remind him that they were in this together.

"I miss Grayden, did you know that? As for you... I'm sure you only miss biting him." Jasper's reply to that was a toss of head that made Lynn laugh despite himself. "And you miss apples. Brynn always brought you the best ones." The big man then dissolved into a wracking coughing fit that left him shaking his head ruefully. "Figures, doesn't it? I'm not even allowed to have a laugh."

A whiskery face and one dark eye turned to regard Lynn in concern—and the king reached down to give that thickly crested neck a pat. "It will improve, everything has to; we all just need some time to heal."

Chapter Six

Donovan was snoring on Vix's chest when sunlight finally filtered into their corner of the cave. The shifts in lighting were minor so deep within the earth, but having spent enough time in the caverns, a man could become attuned to the slightest change. What time was it?

Halfway sitting up, the gunner readjusted the rogue—his arm had gone numb. This jostled Donovan, and one of his sleepy green eyes opened. Well, no time like the present. "I want to go with you," Vix said calmly.

Distantly, there was the clank of spoon on pan, the smell of brewing coffee, and the growling yawn of a dragon from the Great Hall—there were always one or two that preferred to sleep in their Draconic forms.

"You what? No 'good morning' just 'I want to go with you'?" Donovan grunted.

"I'm going. You're right, I don't have to follow orders anymore. I want to go with you and Grayden."

Donovan sighed, nuzzling into Vix's chest

luxuriously… until he felt the hot, raised scar beneath the gunner's tunic. Vix took in a sharp breath at that, and one hand came up to cover the rogue's, stilling him. Rich brown eyes met Donovan's moss-green, a glow in them that was uncertain and vulnerable. A thousand questions went unasked in the count of three breaths, and then Donovan was riding up Vix's shirt.

The rogue's hands plunged beneath the fabric, skating up and down the muscular planes of the dragon's body. When fingertips found the naked scar, they massaged it as he lowered his head, pressing kisses wherever the gunner would let him touch him.

At first, Vix seemed to be contemplating pushing the other man away; but after a time, fear of judgment yielded to desire, and strong hands fisted possessively into Donovan's hair. "Are you sure you want this?" Vix growled, using his grip to force their eyes to meet.

"I want this," Donovan encouraged, unflinching. Situating himself astride the other man's thighs, and ignoring the grip on his hair, the rogue leaned over the bunched fabric of the dragon's shirt to brush their lips together. A rock of his hips wrung a quiet moan of need from Vix… and both men froze.

They might have been in a more secluded portion of the caves, but they were still close enough to be overheard—especially if Vix was as enthusiastic as Donovan thought he might be. "You're loud, aren't you?" the rogue teased, backing off the other man before either of them got more carried away.

"Loud?" Vix rumbled, his dragon showing in his eyes and through the change in his voice.

"Yes. The gods have forsaken me. But... yes." The rogue let the fabric ease back down to cover temptation. "I can't believe I'm saying this, but... later. Later for everything. And you can ask Grayden yourself. If you really want to go, I won't stop you. Now. Breakfast. Let me go get us both something to eat. Then you're going to tell me every detail about what happened by that lake."

The rogue was gone a moment later—and Vix was left completely aroused. "You've got to be joking," he hissed, thumping his head against the travel pack he had been using as a pillow. Donovan didn't play fair.

Copelan had insisted that Tylen stay in human form to keep Brynn warm, which had turned out to be an excellent idea. Clinging to a neck spine, the prince could barely feel his fingers or toes as the blue dragon came in for a heavy landing.

This place—a large clearing in the forest about a

quarter of a mile from the cave entrance—was where all the dragons were taking off and landing from, and the area had become nothing more than a churned, half-frozen patch of mud.

Copelan slipped after he came to a standstill, his hindquarters giving out from numbness. This left Brynn clutching his dark mane and dangling off his shoulder, while Tylen—who had been sitting behind him—ended up tilted off into the muck. Luckily, the younger drake managed to land on his feet, shin deep in mud, sand, and lichen.

"Copelan!" Brynn grunted, letting go of mane to plop down beside Tylen.

The blue dragon swung around slowly, shaking his horned head in alarm. "Are you harmed?" he asked, a concerned hum rising in his chest.

"No, I'm fine. But I'm worried about you. Promise me you'll go rest now," Brynn said. Reaching out, he captured Copelan's muzzle in his hands. Those glowing blue eyes were heavily lidded, and ice was still frozen in thick, dark lashes. "You're cold. You're so cold..."

The prince didn't think, he only acted. Opening the front of his winter cloak, he got a grip at the base of Copelan's horns and pulled that scaly head into the warmth of his body. In any other circumstance it was something he

wouldn't have done for fear of his secret being revealed—
but he was frightened. The higher elevations had been bitter
as was their wont, and the thunderstorm had been icy in
more than one patch—the warm air circulating in from
Tel'aven hadn't been enough to tame it.

Copelan groaned against Brynn; miserable, but
appreciative for even a small amount of relief—and the
prince wished desperately that Grayden was with him, as he
had no idea how to take care of a dragon.

"Let's get you inside, shall we?" Tylen stepped up
behind Brynn, letting his own arms join the embrace as
Copelan shivered where he sat—rump firmly planted in the
mud.

"Copelan!" Maylin called.

Wings rising abruptly in alarm, the big drake tried
to stand and pull away from Brynn—obviously not wanting
his mate to see the state he was in. It also wasn't the best
idea, and he ended up staggering dizzily.

Tylen caught a handful of mane and used it to
steady the other dragon's head until he could balance
himself—only letting go when Copelan relented and shifted
back to human form.

At that juncture, Maylin had struggled across the
field to her mate's side and had both arms wrapped around
his waist. The fear on her face was enough to make Brynn's

stomach clench convulsively. He hated that someone as kind as her had to worry like this. "He's only tired, Maylin, not hurt. He needs a few days off, and I'll see that he gets them." Brynn was trying to put on a brave, confident front, and to be the leader she needed. He hoped being cold and tired was all Copelan's weakness was about. Everyone had been burning the candle at both ends of late, especially the dragons.

"I'm fine… fine, Maylin, I just need to warm up," Copelan wheedled.

Maylin didn't look convinced, but she didn't argue, either. "Alright, then—come in and have some coffee? It might be cold out, but it's the first time I've seen it this sunny in months. It almost makes the storm worth it, doesn't it?"

She was trying to comfort wounded pride and lift the mood, and not for the first time, Brynn found himself glad of Maylin's company. There was something unsinkable about her, and he was grateful for it.

Copelan flashed his mate a sheepish smile just before the group headed for the caverns together—Tylen bearing up under Copelan's left arm, and Maylin under his right. Brynn kept up the rear, watching the forest around them carefully. They hadn't seen any Angelic movement recently, but that didn't mean it wasn't going to happen. At some point the caves would be discovered. There were so many refugees there that it was almost impossible to hide their numbers, no matter how careful they were.

"This is it," Loux said.

Far off down the underground road, a rat squeaked. Grigor frowned. "It's a door. But how do you know it's 'The Door' if you will?"

"Here, this writing," Chell said. Her pale hands traced the grime along the surface of the metal, and as she scraped away the mold with her fingernails, thin, perfectly carved letters appeared. "I can't read it, but the map definitely shows it as being here. The shape of the letters match. This is it."

"It is… this *is* the place..." Loux said quietly, her eyes focusing through the door as if already seeing what was inside. Maybe she was. One never knew with seers.

"Laser engraving," Grigor muttered, then jumped as an old street sign groaned and fell somewhere to their right. "Sort of like arkane etching, but different. Far more precise."

"What does it say?" Chell asked the scholar, not as interested in his comparison as she was the content of the room barred to them.

"Laboratory One," Grigor said breathlessly. "I heard about this place ages ago. I'd nearly forgotten but I've had plenty of sleepless nights down here to think."

"What do you remember?" Chell asked, feeling Sevaren's wide eyes join hers in pinioning Grigor.

Grigor visibly quailed under the intensity, but he couldn't look away from the door. Soon his hands were joining Chell's, tracing the grooves. "They were looking for a cure for the plague. Humanity was dropping like flies, and it seemed that nothing would make it right. People were trying desperate things."

"Desperate is right," Sevaren said darkly. It was if a shadow had fallen over him—and he was reconsidering why he might really have been brought along.

"It's why they did terrible things to the dragons. They thought they were the answer," Grigor continued, shooting Sevaren a sympathetic glance.

"Was it?" Chell asked, hating to demand elaboration when Sevaren was so obviously uncomfortable. Anyone who had marched beside Lynn Broderick during the Liberation knew of the horror dragons had faced—even if they hadn't understood the 'why' beyond human fear and racism. The rogue wasn't a scholar, though, so in this moment she differed to Grigor.

"No. Well, yes and no. There's a lot we lost before

Parliament was formed. People didn't want to think about it. They didn't want to talk about it, and they even went so far as to banish the Tech guild when they found out what had been happening—so a lot of the knowledge died."

"Not all of it." Loux prompted Grigor helpfully.

"No. Not all of it. That's how we got this information. The bugs liberated the scroll from the libraries of Tel'dorath. It fell into my hands at great cost. Then Doc stole it from me before I could even look it over."

Chell smiled wanly to Grigor in the low light. "So I did. But now, the big question remains… how do we open the damned door?"

"If I told you we needed a key, would you have a go at me for stating the obvious?" Grigor sighed.

"No, I'd ask you what sort of key. You're the one who can read old world languages. You tell us." Chell's expression was so desperate it was almost manic.

"Alright, well… yes. Okay." Grigor was fidgeting. Looking the metal paneling over, he patted all around and found nothing even vaguely like a keyhole. Everyone was watching him, and the pressure was mounting for him. When his hand hit the raised rectangle beside the door, he paused. And then leaned closer. Reaching out with his thumb to push away rat and pigeon droppings, he revealed a green, glowing eye. Or at least, it looked like an eye, but touching the surface proved it was made of hard plastic. He gave it a tap for effect. "Old world tech. Great."

"What does that mean?" Chell asked.

"It means..." Sevaren began, miming a sliding motion. "We need a key card."

"A key card? What the hell is that?" Loux frowned. Her eyes looked too big behind her glasses, her hair a filthy, frizzy exclamation around pale face.

Sevaren bowed his head to her, then offered her a cheeky grin, a hint of canine showing. "A metal one by the looks of it. They work on microchips and magnets. It's amazing that the door's wiring has stayed intact this long."

"Unless?" Chell asked warily.

"Maintenance. As we have been guessing, we aren't alone down here," Sevaren replied. "Where do you think the Tech guild went to when they fled?"

"It could be pure luck, and the door was well made?" Chell offered, not even believing herself.

"That... does not make me any more comfortable, Doc," Sevaren finally said. "I hope you aren't planning on using me to open doors in ways that might be... terminal. You'd have better luck finding one of the Guardian's down here and asking nicely."

"She won't," Grigor said sharply, not giving the rogue a chance to answer one way or another. "You're more useful to her alive than dead—even if your death could open this door, which it can't. And asking to parley with a Guardian would be a waste of all our lives. They're fanatical, I hope you know. The worst of the worst of the Tech guild. "

"Key card," Loux said sternly, her hands dancing in the air as she tried to imagine what such a thing looked like. "We need to focus. We need a key card. You're safe, Sev."

"Unfortunately, it seems we're fresh out of key cards," Grigor said gruffly. "I don't suppose we could force the door?" He looked sharply between Sevaren and Chell. "Please tell me that's why you brought an elementalist?" he asked the rogue.

"That is exactly why I brought an elementalist," Chell sighed, not missing how increasingly terrified Sevaren was becoming. He was already claustrophobic as hell. The last thing she needed was for him to lose control, shift into his Draconic form, and try to force his way out of the tunnels. "But the question is… can we persuade the door *quietly?* Because we aren't alone down here, and I don't want to entertain that much company. It's bad enough dodging the patrols." Her gaze fell on Sevaren, who was nervously picking at his filthy robe sleeves.

"I can try?" the dragon offered weakly.

"Let him try," Loux suggested. Her tone an order, not a question.

The rogue queen didn't take offense. She could put aside her pride, and agree that giving an anxiety-riddled magical being a way to redirect his energy was good. Opening the door was a challenge. Dragons liked challenges.

Chapter Seven

The sense of urgency that had been driving Lynn for the last few weeks had returned. If he kept following the Tel'av river, he would be able to lose himself in the rainforests of Tel'dorath. It wasn't a permanent answer, but it would buy him time to take stock of his situation. If he listened, the desert would talk; and if she didn't, her people would.

Seemingly determined to prove that point, the universe had provided Lynn with a caravan—wherein he had managed to barter his winter clothing for something more befitting the desert. It had been a boon for the traders as well; his winter garb was high quality, and would repurpose or resell well. The only thing the king had turned down was the generous offer of trading Jasper for a camel—which the warhorse was blissfully unaware of—but all in all, he felt he had handled the exchange better than anticipated. Trading was a desert art form full of offers, refusals, and counter offers—especially outside of Tel'dorath; and while he was rusty in that regard, he still remembered his mother's language well enough to hold his own.

His time with the nomads had one other pleasant surprise in store for him. It had allowed him to catch wind of the rumors surrounding Skyeford's fall. News traveled fast, and he was counting on that. It also hadn't hurt his morale to hear mention of Grayden, or a man who sounded much like him.

If the healer back in Skyeford—Grigor, was it? — was to be believed, the archmage had survived. And if he had, he was more than likely still doing so. Grayden had lived through far worse more than once, and Lynn fully expected that luck to hold. He didn't get to dwell on thoughts of his partner for long, though. His moment of inattention allowed Jasper to pull the reins through his hands, and the sting of leather sliding against burned palms pulled him out of his reverie. He knew he should probably call a halt for the day—it was getting too hot to ride safely, and he hurt in places he didn't know he owned—yet he kept on.

He couldn't shake the misgivings he had about stopping; and the sensation of being watched was growing—when he saw something from the corner of his eye. At first, he thought it had been the faintest flash of a rainbow glow on the surface of the river. But that was something that only occurred at waterfalls, and his heart sank. He knew what this was. His head turned sharply as a flock of white egrets exploded into the air from the papyrus at the water's edge, making Jasper shy. The traders had to be far behind him now, no doubt on their way to Tel'aven's markets—which only left one option that wasn't based on superstition or conjecture.

Lynn was quick to gather his spooked mount again; but there was a growing feeling of nauseous dread in the pit of his stomach, and it was contagious. Jasper champed at the bit, shimmying as he did before combat—and Lynn could deny it no longer. The Angelic had found him. Instinct told him that they had been trailing him all day, and he hoped the caravan had been spared in favor of more interesting prey; namely himself.

There came a sudden whistling noise above his head, and reflexively he ducked to the side. In that half-heartbeat, a blaze of golden light materialized above him, and the tips of a useless, feathery wing brushed his face. Luckily for him, Jasper's reactions were hair-trigger. The war horse squealed and kicked out with both hind legs at the sound of steel biting through the air—then there was a satisfying thump, followed by an unearthly shout of pain. It would have been gratifying to allow the stallion to swing around and continued the assault, but Lynn checked him instead.

Trying not to look at the Angel crumpled on the ground, the king argued internally with himself whether to fight or flee. But if there was one thing that had been drilled into his head time and again, it was that where there was one Angel, there were more—and weakened or not, they would easily overpower a man with no arkane abilities. They had to run.

Turning a disappointed Jasper toward the shimmering southern horizon, he took a moment to thank the ineptitude of his attackers. Their failure had given him precious seconds to think about his position, and that of his enemy. He could not allow himself to be driven back toward the city, that was certain death; so he had to hope he still knew the land well enough to outmaneuver his opponents before they boxed him in.

"Yah," Lynn grunted—giving his horse free rein, and his ribs a healthy squeeze. As Jasper leaped ahead in a gallop, Lynn heard more alien voices shouting behind him, confirming his theory that he had grazed the edge of a carefully laid ambush. Lucky him. With the mountains closing in on his right, and the river on his left, they would have to cross the water and head southeast. There was a ford nearby that only the goatherds used—a place he didn't think the Angels knew of, and decided it was his best bet.

It was a dangerous wager to make because it was the only choice he had—the enemy could be doing this to drive him exactly where they wanted him—but sometimes a desperate choice was better than refusal to make one. Mercifully, there was no rule that said he had to like anything about his current situation, and he grit his teeth to silence the curses that were struggling their way past his lips. More than anything he agreed with his horse, he wanted to turn and fight—but even weakened Angels were dangerous, and he had promised to find a way to make things right; which was something dead men didn't do.

Punctuating his thoughts, he heard more Angelic blinking in and out of corporeal form in his wake. They were on foot, much to their disgruntlement, and he planned to make them suffer as much as possible.

"Give us the key!" the nearest creature demanded, its lisping voice carrying unnaturally over the sands and echoing off the water.

"What key?!" Lynn called without looking back, feigning ignorance.

One of the monstrosities took another swipe at him that he dodged before leaning forward over Jasper's neck—raising up in the saddle and the stirrups to making himself as light as possible. He then urged the stallion on. Jasper wasn't a racehorse, and he would need every advantage he

could get, especially on desert sands. The ford. They had to
make it to the ford.

"Go on," Grayden said, giving Brynn a gentle
nudge.

"Are you sure I'm not being a bother?" the prince
asked, looking toward the red dragon curled up in the back
of the chamber. Along the sleek scales of her belly, a
handful of newly hatched dragonlings were curled—multi-
colored and glinting in the low light as their tiny chests rose
and fell. One egg remained whole and unmoving, tan and
almost accusatory compared to its adjacent, vibrant
siblings. The queen looked to Brynn, and then nosed the
egg fitfully, her expression concerned.

"You aren't a bother," Tylen replied distractedly, his
hand resting at the small of Brynn's back as he made
respectful eye contact with the mother dragon. Her body
language said she was allowing visitors and interaction, but
the younger drake wouldn't have blamed her if she didn't. A
queen dragon with a fresh clutch was already jumpy. One
that had lost her home and the nest she had been making
was worse. Add in an unhatched egg? That was agony in a
time when dragons were so few. "Besides. You wouldn't
take that hot bath back in Helith, and you barely bothered

to eat—yes, I know I'm being hypocritical—so something social won't hurt. You're allowed to have needs, My Prince; even if they are as simple as spending time getting to know your people, and how you can best support them."

Tylen's words were sincere, but distracted. Interaction with his kin left him constantly on edge. He had never felt like he belonged with other dragons, and he certainly didn't want to misread a situation and fail Brynn. He also had no desire to be identified. Thankfully, most of the dragons in Grayden's employ, and those from Skyeford, had never found themselves near Tel'dorath, estranged as they were from their homeland and kin.

"I've never… seen dragons so small," Brynn answered, sidestepping the conversation about overextending himself. "Are you sure this is okay?" He had seen the queen nosing at her unhatched egg, and he wondered if that meant something was wrong with it.

"I think so," Grayden said softly. He had made the time to bring Brynn here, and he was already glad he had. "Just ask before you do anything that involves touching." He gestured toward the pile of hatchlings and the lone unhatched egg. "Freya, is that the right thing to do?" he raised his voice slightly to be sure the queen knew he was addressing her. Sometimes asking was the best way to go about things—especially with large, ancient beings that could (hypothetically) devour a man in one bite.

"Yes, Archmage," the queen trilled invitingly in reply, lifting a foreleg as Brynn took a few careful steps closer. The twitch of her tail was proud, as was the look in her eye. Her clutch. Her children. "Come," she invited, knowing this was the Crown Prince that she entertained.

While Brynn continued to bow his way nearer to the clutch, Tylen fell back, and Grayden paused at the young drake's side, watching Brynn kneel in the sand beside the hatchlings. "How are you doing, Kid?"

Tylen jumped visibly. He was so concentrated on Brynn—and making sure that everything went well—that he had forgotten about Grayden. "I'm okay," he murmured, head bowed demurely as if he could hide the glow of his eyes. This moment meant a lot to him, to see Brynn accept and show interest in dragons—in people like himself. Brynn would be king someday (if he wasn't now) and Tylen hoped it meant a better future between men and dragons… that was, if Anteas survived.

"Just okay?" Grayden couldn't quite hide the laughter in his tone.

"I… Archmage—"

"—Grayden."

"G...rayden I..." It was hard for Tylen to call the other mage by name. Titles had become ingrained.

"You got a lot more than you bargained for, didn't you? And now that you've got it, you don't have the first clue what to do with it."

"I didn't think that I'd fall in love."

"Look, Brynn's a good kid, the whole monarchy thing notwithstanding. I think you're great for each other. And... I suppose you have some questions, don't you?"

"The sort I can't ask Brynn," Tylen eventually admitted.

"Those would be the ones."

"Should I ask Maylin? What about Copelan? That's what you'd suggest, right?"

"Gods, no. No no no." Grayden laughed quietly. "As much as I hate to admit it, I think it's better if you asked me."

"You'd... do that for me?"

"What, you think we want accidental heirs before we're ready? I can teach you how to keep out of trouble and stay happy. I'm good for that much."

"You'd be willing..."

"Don't make me repeat myself." Grayden groaned, trying not to rub his face. He had agreed to this. He had. This was already his fault, and he would keep his word. He'd known the moment the two laid eyes on each other that this would happen, and this was the price he would pay...

"Okay. So, when?"

"Might be a while, maybe tonight before dinner. Everyone should be getting ready for the trip."

"Do you want me to come along?" Tylen sounded hopeful. He knew he was needed here, but pride was a powerful thing.

"I want you to stay here with Brynn. Someone has to keep him from dying, and whether I like it or not, I suspect that's going to be you. We're already letting you ferry riders back and forth. Don't make me regret—"

"—You'd let a dragon..?"

Grayden crossed his arms uncomfortably to punctuate his growing scowl. "A word of this to anyone and you will be peeling potatoes in the kitchen for the rest of your foreseeable future."

"Yessir."

"No. Don't call me 'Sir' either. I'm not your Archmage anymore." Now he was rubbing his face.

"You'll always be Skyeford's High Archmage, Sir." Grayden winced.

Brynn was aware that Grayden and Tylen were talking, but they didn't seem to be killing each other, so he didn't pay much attention. He was utterly absorbed in the tiny dragon that had crawled into his lap. Its scales were still soft from hatching—softer than an adult's by far. If he had to describe them, the word of choice would have been 'velvety', and the texture had more in common with goat hide. As far as color, the dragonling was a dark crimson, with hints of fuchsia creeping into its neck spines—unlike the more solid red coloring of its mother—and its energy level bordered on frenetic.

As he tried to cradle the surprisingly delicate being to his chest, it was more interested in nibbling on the frizzy waves of his hair; peeping curiously as it explored. Its razor sharp claws were already hardened enough to pick through his shirt, and it used them to crawl up over his shoulder to make itself at home. It was too hyperactive to be still for long, though, and slithering in a quick half-circle around Brynn's neck, it lost its balance and tumbled down onto his thigh; tottering, tail wriggling indignantly.

"Have you named..?"

"Her?" Freya answered, voice soft and sweet despite the lisp caused by her fangs.

Brynn wondered what the dragonling's human form would look like. He knew most dragons took on shades of their true form's coloring in some way—but not all. He suspected Freya's appearance might be surprising. "Yes, have you named her?"

"Not yet. We like to let our young choose the name that best defines them. Egg names are not always kept."

"I see. Being who I am, I must admit that's good to hear. Forgive the more personal question but … Where is your mate? He must be delighted."

The dragonling gave a high pitched shriek of joy when she caught sight of the ribbon binding Brynn's hair; and the prince was left wincing as she batted at it with her talons, the tips snagging into the material.

"He… fell," Freya said, the jolt of sorrow arcing through her visibly—though she was quick to correct it before her children noticed. They were too young to understand language, but sensitive enough to feel her distress.

No longer the center of Brynn's immediate attention, the dragonling finished shredding the ribbon. As it gave way under her weight, she fell to the cave floor again, trumpeting her frustration as she hit the stone with a bony splat.

"Oh…" Brynn replied to the queen, scooping up the unhappy hatchling and cradling her in his lap, trying to distract her from the indignation of her tumble—all the while holding back the instinct to apologize to Freya. He knew how much it had frustrated him when others had done so on behalf of his ruined city.

Idly, Brynn found his fingertips stroking a tiny crimson muzzle, the pad of his thumb tracing nostril and eye ridges as the dragonling halfheartedly teethed at his fingers—her affront forgotten. Her fangs were as sharp as her claws, but she wasn't breaking the skin so much as she was massaging her gums, so he didn't correct her.

"I don't expect you to say that you are sorry, Prince Broderick. It isn't your fault."

"If you ask me not to, M'lady, I won't. But I am sorry for your loss."

"He lives on. In these..." Freya nodded to her clutch. "He died fighting for a better future. A future with peace for our children. That... is worth my grief. If one must lose a mate before their time I suppose this is the best reason..."

"Was he with the Fifth?"

"Yes. He was."

When the hatchling's gumming of his fingers became too enthusiastic, Brynn set her down crisply—and after that eviction, she decided she'd had her fill of the prince. With a peep of offense, she skittered back to her clutchmates, burrowing beneath one of her chubby blue siblings. Already they seemed like such individuals. They had different colors, markings, sizes, and shapes—it was fascinating, and Brynn wondered what the future held for each one. If… they had a future; but that was an idea that he was avoiding entertaining.

Looking up at last, the prince nodded, knowing nothing else could be said. "And forgive me for asking another insensitive question, but that one hasn't hatched." He pointed to the lone egg.

"Sometimes they don't," Freya answered sadly.

"You think this one won't?"

"You tell me, human. Your hands are much more sensitive than my muzzle. The egg is still warm, which means the little one inside is alive. Perhaps, waiting for the right moment?" Her tone wasn't angry, if anything, it was hopeful. She was watching Brynn as inquisitively as he studied the egg in question.

Brynn was close enough that he could touch it if he wanted, and he reached out hesitantly, tapping against the shell with a fingernail—then grinned ear to ear in delight when he felt an answering rap. The queen beside him brightened at that, and the dragonlings that had been feigning sleep turned their attention to their unhatched sibling.

"Do that once more?" Freya asked.

Brynn did. And again, there came an answering knock. Then there was a sharp popping noise that made everyone present jump—and a hole appeared in the egg. After a few heartbeats of intense silence, the egg started to rock. Cracks spider-webbed the tanned surface as a scaly snout poked through, and the prince thought he heard Tylen gasp, but he couldn't tear his eyes away from the scene before him. Brynn wanted to reach out and help the dragonling break free, but he knew better. Part of the hatching process for most birds and reptiles required the effort of escaping the egg. If he tried to help, the hatchling might die... so he waited.

It seemed like it took forever, but eventually a nose worked its way through, and a pointed chin breached the shell's edge—the little one giving a bubbling snort of fluid, and then a lusty shriek of unhappiness from its confines. It was still trapped, and its sharp claws scrabbled at the opening, as it chipped its way to freedom. The queen dragon trilled encouragingly at that, and following her lead, the hatchling's brothers and sisters peeped out as well; cheering on their sibling.

"You see? Freya said with a Draconic smile. "This one was merely waiting for the right time. It isn't every day a human of noble blood witnesses a hatching."

Brynn was completely riveted as the cracks in the egg continued to spread outwards—so much so that he barely noticed Tylen crouching behind him until the dragon's arm wrapped around his waist supportively.

"Blink," Tylen whispered teasingly, "you won't miss it if you do."

The young drake's words made Freya laugh—her relief that she hadn't lost a child as strong as Brynn's curiosity.

Just then, the egg burst open, shards spraying the cave floor and skittering off into the darker corners of the cavern as the dragonling tumbled out protesting— becoming a frail, sticky mess on the cave floor.

What no one expected was for Grayden to stride up calmly and crouch beside the hatchling. Using the lower portion of his cloak, he scooped the squalling thing up and proceeded to rub it until it was free of birth fluid. When he was finished, and he was sure the dragonling was breathing strongly, he rose to lay it at its mother's feet—unfurling its squirming form to her in the dim light of the cave. "There we are, much better," he said matter-of-factly—but when a patch of arkane lantern light hit the hatchling's scales, he frowned. "I've not seen one quite like this before."

Freya regarded the newborn curiously before leaning in to lap at the hatchling's nose and eyes, encouraging the last of the fluids from strengthening lungs. "Nor have I," she admitted between strokes of her tongue.

Bright green eyes stared rheumily up at their mother

and Grayden. The dragonling's scales were multi-hued—red, white, and gold—and the archmage couldn't help but think of a goldfish...

Grayden and Brynn shared a look before Brynn glanced away. The prince had not seen dragonlings this small before, and he'd certainly never seen them hatch—so he wouldn't know if such colorings were normal; but he had also never seen an adult that was brindled in such a way. It was striking, and he wondered if that indicated a birth defect. He prayed that it didn't.

Tylen had gone telling silent, and when Brynn reached down to pat the other boy's hand, he realized he wasn't in the moment with them, he was far away, seeing something else. "Tylen?"

"I've seen this before," the dragon admitted hoarsely, blinking back into the moment.

"Is it bad news?" Brynn asked.

"I... suppose not? Not really. I need a moment, if you will excuse me?" The hand beneath Brynn's was trembling.

"Go if you need to, Kiddo," Grayden said, an unspoken understanding in his gaze and tone.

Brynn frowned. What in the hell was this all about? And he was still asking himself that question as mother and child bonded, and Tylen disappeared before the sea of excited dragonlings could mob him in their joy.

Vix set aside the bowl that Donovan had brought him. It was empty now, as was the old, dented tin cup that he had been drinking coffee from. He'd had worse kit than this, and he was grateful for the full belly, too.

"So what was it like?" Donovan asked idly.

"What was what like?"

"Changing into a dragon for the first time."

"What makes you think I changed into a dragon?" Vix asked, his sense of humor much better after a decent meal.

"Well, what else would you have changed into?" The corner of Donovan's mouth quirked up in quiet amusement.

"What if I'm a werewolf, did you ever think of that?" Vix retorted.

"You're not nearly hairy enough," Donovan chuckled, almost choking on the strip of dried meat he was finishing off.

"Maybe I shave?" Vix was getting into this now.

"With what? Neither of us have seen a straight razor in longer than I care to admit."

"I could use my claws..." Vix whispered

conspiratorially.

"I... your what?" Donovan was looking vaguely alarmed now.

"You know... werewolf claws are as good as straight razors," Vix continued.

"Vix... Werewolves aren't real," Donovan sighed—though he didn't sound entirely convinced.

"Arooo," Vix mimed a quiet howl, and Donovan threw a leather glove at his head—which the gunner ducked, then sobered. "In all seriousness, though..."

"We're capable of that now, are we?" Donovan grunted.

"Maybe." In the distance, the shrieking and peeping of the hatchling's echoed, and a soft smile crossed Vix's face before he looked away from the rogue. There was a shadow of pain behind his eyes. "It felt like I was being torn apart."

"Pardon?"

"Like someone was tearing me apart and putting me back together, one molecule at a time. I was too big, too hot, too... tight—my clothes, my skin, my hair... and then there was blood. Mine. Angels. I... killed. And I think that if there had been any humans, I might have slaughtered them, too."

"That's not too surprising, you were fighting for

your life. Did it ever happen again after that?"

"I woke up naked in the snow, covered in blood. I limped back to base. Kris helped me; my buddies cleaned me up. They asked me what happened, but I couldn't say a word. They didn't press, and I never... never let it happen again."

"Sounds healthy," Donovan deadpanned.

"You're a pile of walking complexes yourself," Vix snapped, but there was no real heat in his tone.

"Tell me something I don't already know."

"Okay..." Vix sighed. "How about... there goes Tylen?" The gunner pointed out into the main hall, and Donovan leaned past the mouth of the cavern they were inhabiting to confirm it.

"Yep."

"Looks like he's running."

"Or walking really fast. Close enough. Huh. Wonder what went down now?" Donovan asked, rising stiffly. He was still exhausted, and it was starting to feel like he never wouldn't be.

"Should we let it go, or find out?" Vix asked. "I don't like meddling."

"I don't think you need to," Donovan confirmed, carefully gathering their dirty dishes. "Looks like the Crown is hot on his heels."

Brynn strode by just as quickly, as if on cue.

"Oh. Lover's quarrel? I really don't want to get involved in that... it never ends well," Vix said uncomfortably.

"Don't I know it." Donovan stretched. "You know, you should get packed if you're coming with us."

"I can come?" Vix asked, visibly relieved.

"Yeah, you said you would, so you are. You think we wouldn't let you?"

Vix frowned at that, turning to give Donovan a suspicious look. Had he played into the rogue's plan? Considering that the other man was trying not to look smug, he suspected he had. Damn.

Chapter Eight

ynn could see the ford ahead. Shimmering in the last of the overwhelming afternoon heat, the water looked like mercury floating above the land. The river was sluggish and lower than usual as the rains had yet to come—which was good news for the king and his mount, as they needed to cross. The problem was getting there.

Before him, an Angel stood, feet planted shoulder width apart, wings raised, sword drawn. Multiple hideous eyes blinked, and its mouth hung open as it gulped raggedly for air. It had achieved what it intended, which was to cut him off from the crossing. He'd made his pursuers chase him through difficult terrain, and they hadn't been in very good shape to begin with; thus, he didn't expect any leniency, and he didn't want it, either. Better to die fighting than on his knees.

"Give us the key," the Angel slurred—an unpleasant sneer turning up the corner of its mouth to reveal blackened, pointy teeth.

Even for Angelic, this lot didn't look like they were prospering. If anything, Lynn expected to see body parts dropping off any minute. "What? Bloody! Key?" he called back over Jasper's braying. The warhorse was pawing at the air in anticipation—he hated the smell of Angels. Always had, and always would.

While his mount pranced in place and continued to voice his displeasure, the king drew his sword. The ring of it leaving the scabbard helped to clear his head. He wasn't certain he was going to survive this encounter, but it would be shameful to fall now. He had to stay alert. Given the slightest of opportunities, he'd run rather than fight.

"Don't be cute, human scum! The key! Give us the key, and we might make your end quick."

"You don't look like you're in the position to call anyone 'scum'. And as I've said before, I haven't any keys. Fresh out, I'm afraid." Lynn could hear the remainder of his pursuers catching up. They were furious with him, and while they might be weakened, he had no arkane abilities to speak of. Four Angels against one man would not end in his favor—so he had to think of something else.

"Rats, all of you! Filthy plague rats!" the Angel blocking the king's path lisped in disgust.

"Looking for the cure, are you? Then I fear you may have to wade amongst the rodents a while longer. I haven't any help to give you, and you chased me damn near to the ends of Anteas. If you ask me, I'd say it looks like you've wasted time you don't have."

They were closing in on him, and they were near enough he could smell them. They lot behind him were desperately out of breath from chasing him on foot—and were as outraged about it as they were inconvenienced by their inability to fly. The more he needled them, the angrier they got. The angrier they got, the more energy they unwisely expended. So far, his not-plan was... mostly working.

Around Lynn, rainbows of light danced across the river. The only way was through. He couldn't turn around, or go back. He thought of Brynn and Grayden and he prayed they were safe. He thought of Skyeford, and his determination grew. He couldn't give up now.

"Be that as it may, what are you going to do, little mortal?" The Angel sounded... concerned as he shifted from an offensive to defensive stance. The fact that he might not be able to stop Lynn if he charged him was slowly dawning on him.

"What do *you* think I'll do?" Lynn asked quietly, watching the monstrosity do mental gymnastics.

The Angel blinked at him with three eyes, and another three followed belatedly after. Making a rude hand gesture, Lynn then dug his heels into Jasper's sides—not that the warhorse needed any encouragement—and together, horse and rider made their last stand; Lynn leaning to the side of his mount, blade on the upswing while Jasper laid his ears back, teeth bared as he snaked his neck.

When the warhorse's armored breastplate slammed into the Angel's hip, there came a seemingly disembodied blast of arkane power. An enormous shadow blocked out the sun, and horse and rider went sprawling down the embankment into the ford—Lynn thrown directly into the river as Jasper collapsed in a tangle of legs and braying outrage.

The last thing the king saw before he was struck hard in the head was the flash of green scales and ivory fangs… and a surprised Angel going down a dragon's gullet headfirst. Then the world grew dim around the edges, Lynn's body finally registering the trauma of a slap from a dragon tail. Unearthly screams were muffled as he sank beneath the shallow water, and then everything was cool and quiet.

Sevaren slid toward the floor, Loux struggling to shoulder up under him heroically—but in the end, the two still ended up on the grimy asphalt. Giving up, Loux tucked herself under the dragon's chin, and her open palm came to rest poignantly over his pounding heart. Everyone was so weary, and it was pitiful to behold.

Grigor kept having to fight the urge to examine Sevaren. As a healer, he was worried for someone in his care. As a man, he was terrified of the situation. Having a dragon in their midst had given him some unspoken comfort… and if Sevaren dropped dead, he didn't know what he'd do. What *they'd* do.

"Damn," Chell hissed, fingertips trailing over a perfectly clean—if toasty to the touch—metal door. The plus side of fire magic was the way it had burned away the filth. The bad part was that the rogue was growing increasingly concerned about the inner workings of the door. If they damaged the mechanics, they wouldn't ever be able to open it, proper key or no. "Stop. Just stop. There's nothing we can do now. Rest up, and then we can get out of here. We know what we need."

"You think we will ever be able to find this place again?" Loux asked, her voice ragged. "We've been down here for an age. Even I have lost track."

Absently, Sevaren stroked Loux's hair as he slumped back against the moldy wall. "I second that," he added, voice a low growl. It was costing him to maintain his human form—and his control.

"Of course we will," Chell said sternly.

"And what if we've notified everything and everyone down here with us that we've been toying with Forbidden Doors?" Grigor asked the rogue.

"Why, we just deny it. The cameras don't work anymore... I checked." Chell looked smug.

"I think that the denizens down here—the ones that we have yet to see—would have to be blind and deaf to miss what I've done." Sevaren sighed. "Let alone believe a rogue. You know the Tech guild didn't take kindly to the betrayal that drove them down here."

"On that, I agree, but as for being loud? It wasn't, I promise you. The first time I was down here trying to open doors, one of my colleagues was thinking... more along the line of sledgehammers," Chell said. Judging by the sadistic pleasure in her tone, she was wishing her current crew had gone the more physical route.

"He carried a sledgehammer down here?" Loux asked, sounding surprised at resourcefulness and fortitude. They had been crawling on their bellies in some portions of the underground, and she couldn't imagine squeezing a physical body plus a sledgehammer into too many of them.

"She," the rogue corrected.

"Gods preserve us," Sevaren groaned, interrupting

Chell's story. "We have to get out of here. I don't know how much longer my nerves will hold."

"Seconded," Grigor grunted, finally giving in to his worry and crouching beside Sevaren to check his pulse. The dragon was not eating enough to keep up with the calories he was expending, and the last thing they needed was for him to lose control of the arkane... or his physical form, for that matter. Death was always a potential consequence of arkane exhaustion, but was, sadly, the lesser evil in their current situation.

Tylen leaned against a particularly hearty set of tree roots that framed the mouth of the caves, his expression unreadable. Beside him, Brynn stood, not looking at the dragon, but not ignoring him either. Unspoken words loomed between them, and the tension was palpable. A sentry had passed by a few minutes ago, but now it was quiet again—most likely in deference to Brynn's position.

If the prince walked as if he wished to be left alone, his desire was usually respected. If he acted like he didn't want to speak, it went much the same. At times that was a boon, but at others it was damning—like now. Where did one begin with an upset dragon? He didn't even have the first clue as to what had triggered Tylen to being with.

Brynn tried not to let the silence eat at him, though, and instead of pacing as he would have liked to, he perched on the arch of a dry root, pale face turned up to the sun. He was still exhausted, and judging by Tylen's recent almost-outburst, the dragon felt much the same. "Can I ask about it?" Brynn murmured, breath steaming with each word despite the quickly warming earth.

Tylen didn't answer, but the shake was back to his hands. Without looking, Brynn reached out until he could twine his fingers with the dragon's. Tylen glanced down to him—giving him a smile that Brynn felt more than saw.

"I don't know if I should say anything..." The dragon's voice was little more than a whisper.

"Why not?"

"I don't want to break this—to break everything. I'm afraid this illusion of peace—this something *good*— will shatter once you know."

"I understand that fear. But please believe that you don't have to tell me anything you don't want to." Brynn gave the dragon's bigger hand a squeeze—and eventually it was returned; Tylen's expression softening as if it hadn't occurred to him that Brynn would want to be there for him, for *this*.

"You would know what it's like, wouldn't you?" Tylen stated rhetorically. The revelation last night had gone

133

unspoken between them, and it didn't seem that it would change how Tylen felt about Brynn. "So, tell me where to start?"

"At the beginning, naturally." Brynn gave Tylen's hand a tug until the dragon sat down beside him. The prince still worried that he might be listening to his heart too much—that there was a strong chance that Tylen was a Separatist. But he also believed in the dragon in a stubborn, unshakeable way. He just had to listen with his heart, and the truth would come out—and it probably wasn't as bad as he or Tylen feared.

Tylen bowed his head for a moment, then glanced up as if finding the place he wanted on a book page. "At the beginning? Then I would have to start with my family. Specifically, my brother. Do you remember when I spoke of him?" Tylen asked.

"I do. You said your mother was afraid she was barren, so when she had a small clutch at last—it was a triumph. You also mentioned that she was overprotective because of that."

"Rayen was a runt. He looked much like that dragonling back there, and that *does* mean something— especially to the humans who experimented on dragons. That coloration is a bone of contention among my flight."

"But why? Does color even matter? I see plenty of

mated pairs that don't stick to their own color when choosing a partner, and multi-colored clutches like Freya's." Brynn was frowning, obviously disturbed by such an overtly racist concept.

"Multi-colored scales mean human blood somewhere in the dragon's parentage. And where I was from, that was a death sentence. It isn't quite that extreme anymore. Now, a dragon like that would just be ostracized—but for someone of my... standing to carry human blood, or even be accused of it? Even today it would be horrifying; especially for my mother."

"So Freya's dragonling has human blood somewhere in its lineage?"

"Yes. The little one does." Tylen's expression was solemn.

"So it would..."

"If humanity could have gotten their hands on that dragonling fifteen years ago, it would have died down in the laboratories of Sine. Probably horribly."

Brynn made a sound of disgust. "I don't understand how anyone can do that to a living being."

"They were desperate, and misguided," Tylen said. "Have you noticed that you don't see any dragons that look like that anymore? There are none, because they were hunted to extinction by human scientists, and our flights became so fearful to associate them that they were pushed to the fringes of our society. It's a garbage set of assumptions to make—not all dragons with human blood in their veins appear as that dragonling does. Some don't even know they have human blood at all, and their families work hard to keep it that way. Dragons are genetically diverse—so a clutch doesn't always look true to immediate flight or parents. Which, naturally, that has led to some destructive secrets over the years."

"But why? Why Half-dragons? Why are they better or worse for experimentation than a full-blooded dragon?" The prince gave Tylen's hand another squeeze, seeing the way he was drooping. This was not a cheerful conversation.

"Because Half-dragons... had human blood, and were immune to the plague," Tylen admitted grudgingly. "Full blooded dragons... If you gave their blood—or a derivative of it, like a vaccine—to anyone other than another dragon, their internal organs would explode. Half-dragons are more... compatible, if you will."

Brynn stared at Tylen as the true horror registered. "So, they used Half-dragons to manufacture a vaccine?" The prince was aware of some old world technology. He knew that in the old world they had given injections to people that created immunity against communicable diseases.

"A cure, and a vaccine. All those who live now owe their existence to Half-dragon blood. Unfortunately, after the Crisis much of that knowledge was lost. After the fall, science struggled on. It grasped things more dimly, and it certainly became more barbaric."

Brynn processed this for a second longer. "Let me get this straight. You're saying your brother got kidnapped, and they took him away to experiment on him, and he died."

"Him, and my mother. Mother escaped, but she couldn't save Rayen, and after what they did to her, she was totally barren."

Brynn's horror grew. "No wonder she was so fearful of humans."

"No wonder," Tylen confirmed, leaning into Brynn. The other boy looked pensive. "Do you want me to stop talking? This is... dark."

Brynn shook his head slowly. "Understanding you, and what your family has been through, is part of Anteas' history. A monarch who doesn't know the rounded truth of history, who doesn't learn from it? They'll just keep making the same mistakes—which Skyeford can't afford."

"But how... does it make you feel about me?" Tylen asked hesitantly.

The dragon was stubborn and slow to speak of how

he felt, but he was attempting with Brynn. He wasn't as subtle as he thought he was—and it was endearing. "No different than before," Brynn admitted. "But it makes me see how much work remains to be done—assuming we somehow survive current circumstance."

"Then you understand..." Tylen said shyly, hesitantly. "How I feel about you?"

The words stunned Brynn into silence, and he turned at the waist to look up to Tylen. Golden hair was backlit brilliantly in the morning light, and the dragon's honey-gold eyes had taken on a glow that conveyed the strength of the emotions he was experiencing. Simply put, he was stunning, and while he wasn't human, he was still everything Brynn had ever ached for on cold lonely nights—the sort where he cried himself to sleep, believing that no one could love someone like him.

Leaning up, Brynn's grip on Tylen's hand slipped until he was only clasping two fingers—and then he pressed their lips together before he could lose his nerve, heart racing. Love... this was love, wasn't it?

Tylen wasn't surprised, or at least, he didn't seem to be as he leaned into the kiss; tilting his head until warm, silky hair fell into the prince's lap—lips parting so that they could share a breath. Relief. There was so much relief in their every motion, and Brynn had to admit that he was glad this hadn't gone as he feared it might.

"No matter what happened in the past, I still want to be right here," Brynn whispered when they pulled back, pressed forehead to forehead, lips brushing as he spoke. "I think... I love you."

Tylen's only response was to scoot closer, the hand Brynn wasn't holding reaching out to clasp the prince's upper arm—thumb rubbing reassuringly.

Brynn had to fight back tears as the bands of anxiety that had twisted around his heart, loosened. "Tell me? What... made you choose me, Tylen? Why did you pick me to talk to, to hold... to understand? Not that I'm not grateful, but you could have had anyone; and someone with fewer issues, certainly." Brynn sighed tiredly. "Someone who wasn't human."

Tylen finally guided Brynn into a proper hug, tucking him under his chin so he could bury his nose into the other boy's unruly hair. "No one else would be you, Brynn. Your scent, your touch, your eyes, your heart. No one can take your place. Did you know that the moment a young drake meets someone he will be with for the remainder of his days, he knows? It's magic. And who am I to argue with that?"

"You're just saying that," Brynn said, burying his face into the folds of Tylen's robes, letting the dragon rub his back gently. Even if what Tylen said was a flight of fancy, it was a sweet one—to think that that magic brought them together appealed to a place deep inside that had been devoid of hope for weeks now.

"I'm really not. I certainly wouldn't have chosen a human partner on my own. But I did. Love is not something you can scientifically reason, or even quantify. All I know is that when our worlds were falling apart, I found you. And if all these bad things are going to happen anyway? It's a little easier to face them with you at my side."

Brynn fell silent, taking comfort from Tylen's closeness. He didn't know what more to say, but sometimes silence was nice. There were things that only touch could express the depth of. He wasn't angry when Tylen finally interrupted, though.

"Would you like to go hunting with me?" The dragon asked, peering down at Brynn.

The question was an uncharacteristic one, and the prince didn't quite know what to make of it. It took a lot of trust for Tylen to ask—Brynn knew how the other boy felt about eating meat. Unfortunately, he also knew how important it was to Draconic growth and health. Grayden had told him so.

"... When we return, we could cook up whatever

you want from my kill," the dragon bargained when Brynn didn't immediately respond; feeling he might need to sweeten the deal.

Brynn felt bad saying yes to any activity that seemed frivolous or fun. Recreation—even the necessary sort—didn't seem like something he should pursue when his land was in shambles... yet he found Tylen's enthusiasm contagious. "I suppose... I've wanted to get out for a while," Brynn admitted, pushing back against the heaviness surrounding his heart. Tylen had to eat, and more supplies were always needed; so it was a win-win situation.

Vix looked like he wanted to be anywhere but in the same room as Maylin—who was doing her best to appear non-threatening. Since admitting what he'd always known, the gunner felt like he stood out indelibly. Most of that self-consciousness was in his head, but he was still intimidated—yes, even by Maylin. Lately, he worried he might be making up what was happening to him, thus he felt he had no right to talk to other dragons, let alone ask them for help. He needed it, but he didn't know where to begin.

Before, it had been simple for him to blend in around so many arkane capable people—dragons included.

A dragon might believe Vix didn't want to talk about, or use, his Draconic form, and a human would never notice unless he shapeshifted—which Vix refused to do. Basically, he had been hiding in plain sight his entire life. Now... this? This was the hard part, the coming out of his shell. At least Donovan hadn't left his side.

Said rogue now stood unflinchingly beside him, hand on his shoulder—and Vix's mouth went dry as he sought the right words. The comfortable, peaceful expression on Maylin's face made her seem so innocent, and he didn't want to saddle her with his problems. Or worse... see the hate twist her features when he admitted his parentage.

Mind, he couldn't imagine Maylin hating him—it seemed impossible for a woman so kind—but he knew how most dragons felt about Half-dragons. He'd seen dragons kill their own kind, even their own young, over the smallest trace of human blood. Others he'd seen chased away or abandon outside of human cities... which, deep down, Vix suspected was the explanation for his own fate.

He didn't remember much of his life before the Academy. Only being hungry, cold, and alone. Within those heavily structured halls, it had been much the same. The time at the lake when he had shifted forms... it was the closest he had ever been to recalling who he was, or where he was from. He wasn't even sure 'Vix' was his real name. There was part of him that didn't want to remember—not when, for the first time, he thought he might have a shot at happiness—but here he was, risking it all like an idiot.

"Vix?" Maylin prompted softly.

The gunner realized he had been staring at her for a while, and he immediately gave her a bow of apology. "I'm sorry. I have so many questions, and I don't know where to turn."

"If I was human, this is when I would tell you to get in the queue," Maylin laughed quietly. "And before you tell me that I look too busy, let me assure you, I have plenty of time."

"See, that's just it. You have a lot of time to hate me if you don't like what I have to say. And I... gods I'm scared. I don't know who else to ask. I mean, you tolerate the hatchling, I've not heard one bad word about it from anyone here. But what if... what if I was like *that*?"

Maylin's hand paused where it was hovering— about to give the officer's quarters arkane heater a smack. Her green eyes grew increasingly serious as she studied him. "I thought you knew..." she said, tone mildly scandalized.

"You thought I knew what?"

"I thought you were a dragon, Vix. That you simply

didn't want to shift forms around us because you were the private sort. I wouldn't have guessed that you had human blood."

"Maybe I'm wrong," Vix said, wincing.

Maylin followed through, giving the arkane heater a hard strike with the heel of her hand—and the stubborn piece of machinery began to tick its way back to life.

"You're not wrong," Maylin said quietly. "It's how you survived being so grievously wounded. You are an elementalist, then. You chose to be among the armored division, but what is your element to call? Do you know?" She was regarding him like he might rattle if she shook him.

"Water. I think… it's always been water."

"That *is* a rare thing. Have you spoken to Grayden about it?"

"Gods no! I… didn't even tell anyone at the Academy. I didn't want to be a mage. They thought I was more or less a null, and when someone put a gun in my hands it was like I was born to use it, so it never came up."

"When was the first time you shifted forms?"

"A few years ago. I… don't remember much. I'm sorry, I keep saying that, but it's true."

"I could ask Grayden if he could find your papers. They're locked to you, but if he requests them at the

Academy… I'm fairly certain they would end up in his hand—even now, at the seeming end of the world."

"Do you really think he would do that for me?" Vix asked.

"Are you sure you really want to know the truth?" Maylin countered.

"It would change everything forever." Vix fidgeted.

"Yes. It would. But I think it's already too late for that," Maylin apologized.

There was a long moment of silence, and then the gunner nodded helplessly—looking over his shoulder to Donovan and away from Maylin. The rogue gave him an encouraging wink, which further flustered him; but this time, Vix found the right words. "You're right. I lost control the first time. I need to know how to keep that from happening again. I could hurt people."

"Yes. You can. Strong emotions drive dragons—sometimes it even pushes them to destruction. You might be able to ignore your abilities and passions for a little while longer, but in the end, they will catch up to you. It's a matter of whether you choose to embrace them and prosper, or ignore them and let them drive you to ruin. I know what your heart says—that you wish none of this had ever come to pass, that you would be anyone else, anywhere else, if you could. But I am a firm believer that we are exactly where we are meant to be, when we are meant to be there. I also believe that we come to decisions exactly when we are meant to make them.

"What she means..." Donovan muttered, fingers stroking the back of Vix's shoulder, "Is that this is the perfect time to ask. It's hard, it's scary to admit what you don't know—but if anyone can help you learn to handle what's happening, it's her. She's your family, your kin. You have a chance to get something back that you lost before you knew you had it."

"I don't know if I'm the best dragon for the job, but I promise I will try my best to help you. And what I don't know, Copelan will..." Maylin reached up and took Vix's big hand in her smaller one, tugging him down to sit by her. "You have nothing to fear from me. I lost a sister to the laboratories for the same reason you found yourself in the Academy. It would be worse than hypocritical for me to call your parentage into question."

Slowly, Vix let himself be guided down, his heart racing, and he was grateful when Donovan took a seat behind him. He had no idea why the rogue seemed to enjoy their time together so much, but he had a sneaking suspicion that Donovan's choices weren't entirely based in ulterior motive.

Chapter Nine

ynn rolled onto his belly, wheezing desperately for air. Hands clenching into fists in the sand, he retched up what felt like half of the Tel'av river; and when he could finally breathe again—he realized he had gone from the frying pan to the fire. A scaly, clawed hand had wrapped itself around his waist, and the talons attached to it were like sabers.

Shit.

"Tell me why I shouldn't kill you. Give me one good reason," a heavily accented female voice rumbled in his waterlogged ear.

The scent of hot arkana and the natural smoky tang of dragon filled the king's nostrils; and as he tried to find his voice and think—the claws around him tightened painfully.

A dragon. He couldn't see her properly because his vision was blurry, but he vaguely remembered her from before he lost consciousness.

Coughing again, Lynn managed to clear his throat

enough to rasp out the word "Enough!" The command in it seemed to give the dragon holding him pause. He was dropped again, this time the claws leaving his frame entirely. "I appreciate your help, but enough. I've had enough." The king pushed himself up onto one arm, trying to ignore the feeling of sand caking to the water on his body. "And if I were you, I wouldn't eat me. I'm far too sandy, and your teeth would ache for a week. Kill me? Maybe, but why dirty your talons?"

The bright sun was making halos in his vision, and through the corona, Lynn could make out emerald green scales and brilliant green eyes. Slitted pupils dilated and contracted as the beast in question considered his response, and claws drummed once on the hard-packed earth of the riverbank.

"You have a point. But who are you to command one such as me?"

"Position aside, it's common courtesy to not kill and eat someone before you've been introduced. Especially if you already spoiled your appetite with something as distasteful as an Angel."

"A little bold to assume, don't you think?"

"Nothing good was ever accomplished by a man who gave up before his time."

"Time, what would you know of it, human? I ask

again, why should I let you live? Give me one good reason."

"You're already letting me live," Lynn said. Forcing himself to his feet, he only stayed upright for a heartbeat before he staggered, falling onto his hip in the sand. He felt more than heard the low growl of Draconic frustration at his response—and the thrum of arkane magic lashing the air around him as the dragon's temper rose. Still, he plowed ahead. "So, I suppose it's more along the lines of what you plan to do with me," he told the sand, having trouble lifting his head. "But I can assure you that I'm valuable enough that the Angelic chased me all the way to your doorstep, through a sandstorm no less, so I might be of some use to you."

"I have no use for humans, the lot of you disgust me."

"And you have every reason to say that." Lynn said, trying to stand again. This time he did find his feet—and with great effort drew himself up to this full height, wiping the mud and sand from the side of his face to better regard the dragon. She was beautiful. There was still river water dripping from her light green mane, and it wreathed her narrow muzzle and delicate horns in a glittering crown. "But you did save me, for which I am grateful..." Peering up through the dirty tangles of his hair, something tickled at the back of the king's mind. A memory, half-formed and lost in the murk of time. "Empress."

At that the queen had a sudden seat on her haunches, the tip of her tail twitching as she considered Lynn. Tilting her head quizzically, she leaned closer; nostrils fluttering as she scented the big man before her. "You are one of the desert's children, are you not?" Some of the defensiveness had gone out of her tone, and it seemed as if she, too, was recalling something from an age long past.

"I see there is nothing hidden from you. Yes. I am hers." Lynn held out a hand toward the dragon's muzzle, offering it palm up. He did not flinch or look away, and for a time both man and beast were still. When the dragon lowered her head the rest of the way, it was to nuzzle into his palm, breathing him in... and as the memory overtook her, she pulled away with a snort.

"We should go. Your mount most likely lives, but has run off. Hurry. The longer we stay, the greater the chance that those monsters will return in number." Lowering her shoulder to Lynn, she indicated that he should climb onto her back.

Lynn paused at that, but only for an instant—then he offered her a polite bow and clambering up her elbow, which she used to lift him to the smooth scales of her withers. It was a space on dragons that naturally made a place for a rider, and such a position put Lynn in front of wings so her flight would not be hampered.

"Do you remember me now, Empress?" he asked politely, clasping a neck spine for balance as the dragon hefted her hindquarters from the ground. Her motions were more urgent than they had been before.

"It has been a very long time, Child."

"It has. But I'm home now."

"Just in time for the rains, as it should be. All hearts return as the desert wakes."

"I fear I am here because it is the end."

"No end comes without a beginning, Child. But you must have your eyes open to see it, and they cannot be clouded by tears of grief to do so."

"You speak truth."

"You speak through pain."

"Pain is part of mortality."

"And like mortal lives, pain is not forever."

"You are wise, Empress. If only my heart came to you empty of burden—as it once was."

"You are not so blind. Have faith, child of the desert, have faith."

And then she was launching herself into the air, and Lynn was scrambling to hold on with wet hands.

At least, he thought drolly, his hair and clothing would be dry when they reached their destination—the sun was merciless despite the rain clouds building in the distance.

Brynn rested his hand on the shoulder of Tylen's Draconic form. Spines and fins were tucked tight to the dragon's body as his head lowered and he nosed at the shrub in front of him. He had all the instincts... and no drive. He had already refused to hunt from the air; but if what Grayden had revealed to Brynn was correct, the prince could understand why. Tylen was new to flying... and to a lot of things—yet he had already improved a great deal, and would continue to.

Some of that had been with Brynn's help. When Grayden had finally relented and allowed Tylen to carry passengers, the young mage had stolen away with Brynn to practice at the clearing—repeating takeoffs and landings until he had it down to a science. Tylen's hunting skills, however, seemed to be awkward at best; but no one could improve in every direction at once.

"I'm not any good at this."

"You survived in the deserts of Sine for long enough, did you not hunt there?" Brynn asked. Rubbing a glittering patch of scales, he was rewarded by Tylen tilting his head in pleasure—and if it reminded the prince of a dog with an itch, he remained wisely silent.

"I felt shame over it. Eating meat meant I was a dragon, and being a dragon meant being a tool for humanity to use. I wanted... to be human. I wanted to be accepted and have worth. But then I'd get desperately hungry and eat the first thing I stumbled on—which left me feeling guilty until the next time I got frantic for a meal."

"But you have to eat meat. You're not meant to be a vegetarian. I'm sure you can make a meal out of many things, but to grow..."

"You're as bad as Maylin," Tylen murmured, looking chastised.

Brynn laughed quietly, patting the dragon's golden shoulder again. "You need to eat to grow strong. You're a mage, having some reserves isn't a bad thing."

"It feels wrong... because I like it. I'm bad at it, but I like it."

"What, hunting?" Brynn asked.

Tylen nodded his scaly head, "What about you?"

"I'm okay at it. Father insisted I learn, so I know the basics. He was very proud of my first stag. I... well, I used to have the antlers on the wall at the entrance to my rooms. I hung cloaks there, but I guess that's gone now."

"It is," Tylen said. "Yet I'm sure we will find your father, and when this nightmare is over, you will hunt with him again. Ella has taught you new skills, and I have no doubt you are now twice as deadly as you once were."

"I wish I could share your optimism," Brynn said, swallowing past a lump in his throat.

"Forget your grief for now. Take what you know how to do and use it to help your people. There are many mouths to feed within the caves, and game is roaming further afield. How about I help you carry the kills, and we take what we can? I'm not a good hunter, but I'm strong and I can fly with you on my back and several deer in my talons." Tylen curved his neck so that he could make eye contact with Brynn, one golden pupil dilating and contracting as he scented the air again.

"I suppose that would work," Brynn said. Any distraction was a welcome one—he couldn't keep focusing on his own pain. "And I'm here hunting with you, aren't I? At least you're with a friend if you *must* do something you don't like to."

"*Should* do," Tylen corrected. "And I would say so." He gave the other boy the Draconic equivalent of a grin. "Maybe it's not so bad to like feeding, as long as I'm hunting for you?" The dragon found the idea less onerous when he could convince himself that his strength and health were needed by someone else.

"But. One stipulation." Brynn held up a scolding finger in front of Tylen's snout. "You have to eat your fill first. Then we hunt for Skyeford. You might have fed your human form this morning, but your Draconic one? You look… drab. And skinny." Brynn tried to keep his tone light as he poked at visible ribs. A dragon that didn't eat and was growing at the same time, well, he'd seen mages drop dead from less… and he was worried.

A dragon's scales could lose their color if they were stressed or malnourished, and Brynn wasn't an expert, but he knew that Tylen's luster was gradually fading. Times were hard on everyone, yet the other boy had worked his way into Brynn's heart—which he seemed to have a knack for—and now the prince feared losing him more often than he wanted to admit. "Please? I can't handle one more death."

"Very well. But only because you asked so nicely," Tylen agreed, snorting as he caught the scent of rabbits.

"Fine. Then that brings me to the most important question: what do you like to eat?" The set of Brynn's jaw was borderline mulish.

"Truthfully?" Tylen asked. "I was hatched in a temple near the Tel'av river, and I love fish. Ocean fish, fresh water… it doesn't matter what sort, I love them. I also like to swim, but that is neither here nor there.

"Are you sure you aren't a water dragon?" Brynn teased, mood taking an upturn as quickly as it had crashed.

"Ask me to go swimming sometime, and find out," Tylen rumbled.

"Fine, maybe I will; and all the fish are below the ice now, so how about venison?"

Tylen lunged, jaws closing around the buck's throat—his bite very nearly decapitating. Wings flared up possessively as he pinned his ears back, his eyes closed tightly against his disgust at what he had done. Even if its head was nearly off, instinct had the dragon strangling his prey until it finally stopped kicking. When the last shudders left the beast's body, he let go and blinked his eyes open again—his guilt obvious in their golden depths. The buck fell to the ground with an accusatory thump, the snow and mud beneath it staining pink from the blood still seeping from its neck.

Brynn had stood well back. Tylen as a dragon was clumsy in some ways, and frighteningly precise in others. When he was fully grown, he would probably be terrifying; but even as a young adult he was powerful, and Brynn found it hard to swallow past the nervous lump in his throat. He loved Tylen. He did. But adjusting to the fact that he was a dragon—and wrapping his head around every aspect of that—could be jarring at times. "It's okay. Tylen, it's okay. That's yours. Yours to eat. It's important for you to eat." Brynn reminded, voice low and soothing.

There was a stack of dead animals at the edge of the forest. Tylen had been saving the last kill of the evening for himself—perhaps because it was the hardest for him to justify—and Brynn had relented on his previous requirement. It was wisest to pick his battles, and accept whatever ground he could gain.

Tylen growled at the prince as he approached, the sound ending in a distressed rattle. Nostrils fluttering, the drake moved to stand over the dead beast uncertainly—caught between instincts and emotion.

"It's yours, Tylen. All yours. Go on. Don't be sad. I know you won't waste anything," Brynn crooned. For an instant, he thought Tylen might attack him, but as the prince placed a bare hand on that hot, scaly neck—uncertain rumbling became an inviting trill.

Then Tylen was backing away, nosing the dead deer toward Brynn's feet, and the prince had no idea what to do. Crouching to examine the kill—which he suspected Tylen was expecting him to—he allowed himself a smile as the dragon gave him a hopeful chirp. "You'd feed a mate like this, wouldn't you?"

The fact that Tylen would do something he hated to protect and care for Brynn... it allayed some of the prince's fears, while highlighting how easy it was to misinterpret cultural gestures. Being a mate, being a lover; it meant something different for dragons. "Well, I can't eat this unless I cook it. Why don't you save a piece for me, and eat the rest?"

Tylen was all dragon in the moment, lost inside himself, and the conflict showed in those gold eyes. Chest heaving, legs braced, he hovered—torn between two vastly different sets of instincts.

"You were never meant to be a soldier, were you? It's okay. I'm not cut out for it, either. I might enjoy hunting, but I'm already tired of war."

Tylen crouched in reply, the motion putting him close enough to nuzzle against Brynn's trouser leg. In response, the prince clasped a horn and guided Tylen's snout back toward the kill. "Go on." He thumbed a neck spine companionably. "This is yours. Remember?" The dragon was gory, his mane splattered in mud and blood— and Brynn still loved him all the same.

Brynn was standing at the edge of the fire pit while Copelan and Vix showed him how to spit the haunch Tylen had left for him. Grayden's stood several yards away, back to the fire as he chatted with Tylen. There was enough distance between the mages and the trio at the fire that neither group could hear what the other was talking about—and Grayden planned to keep it that way.

"I… certainly hadn't thought of that," Tylen muttered.

"And that is exactly why I'm warning you," Grayden watched Tylen squirm while trying to look like he wasn't, and he had to fight down his own amusement.

"What of the herbs he needs?"

"Now that I know that issue hasn't been addressed, I can see to that before I go. There's no need for him to be miserable when we have multiple skilled healers and herbalists at our disposal. We even have a few among our numbers who know how to work old world medicine and technology."

"I… please don't tell him we discussed this."

"I won't. Tylen, just… I can't believe I'm saying this, but for the love of the gods, be careful?" The archmage had a hard time imagining the dragon treating the

humans around him with anything less than kid gloves—
especially Brynn—but he was still moved by a parental
need to be certain.

"I promise."

"Good enough. That's the best I can hope for in the
face of youthful enthusiasm."

"Archmage, are you grilling the suitor of our
illustrious prince?" A warm voice interjected.

Grayden swiveled just in time to see Rose hiding a
laugh behind her hand, and then to Sarah as she strode into
the room after the other woman. "Of course!" He answered
smartly.

"I thought you didn't want to be a father," Sarah
teased—throwing something at Grayden that he caught
with a practiced flick of his wrist. It was another pack of
cigarettes.

"I have absolutely no desire to… where did you
scare these up?" The archmage overcame his exaggerated
insult as he studied the paper carton.

"You're doing what fathers do, Archmage, it's
unmistakable. You might be a stepfather, but you are
raising a child. Or two. Or a thousand," Rose said
pleasantly. "And you can thank me. I was down in the
bazaars for a time, and there's more where that came from."

Grayden gave Sarah a mock fierce look that hinted

good-naturedly that she should let the subject drop—then turned to face Rose. "You certainly know how to give an old soldier hope, Lady Forscyth." He offered her a rare grin.

"Maybe I do. I also hear you're in need of an herbalist."

Grayden arched a brow.

"I was listening in," Rose bit her lip in amusement, her hand falling limply to her side.

"Formidable and resourceful—I never even knew you were here. I don't suppose you missed your calling as a rogue?" Grayden gave the flustered young woman a wink. Her hair was mussed, and so was Sarah's… and he knew. Looking back and forth between the two women, he found he wasn't entirely surprised, either.

"Did your recon pan out?" Grayden prompted, giving Tylen a tilt of chin that indicated that their previous discussion was over. The dragon shifted gears gratefully, and soon he was sitting down at the empty ammunition crates that served as a makeshift table and chairs.

Rose hopped onto the same crate as Sarah, while Grayden, and Tylen made themselves as comfortable as possible on the remaining two. Brynn was still distracted at the fire, and Grayden wanted him to stay there—or at least, be out of ear-shot. The prince suffered enough survivor's guilt as it was.

Ella and Donovan were out, doing… whatever it was that they did. The tracker had been busy preparing for the scouting party's departure, and the addition of Vix to the team meant she had to scramble for more supplies. Grayden could fill her in later. Donovan? The archmage just wanted him as far away from him as possible. Grayden's plans operated on uncomfortably slim margins of error, and the rogue was a catastrophe waiting to happen.

Rose ran her fingers through her mussed hair, then leaned forward to rest her elbows on her knees before she spoke. She wasn't always quite sure of where to start with something so dire, and had been hoping to never have to face this sort of situation in her lifetime—let alone find a way through it. She didn't get a choice, though. Grayden had to know.

"The Angels are getting bold. They roam the streets of Belden and Gent like they own them, and anyone who gets too near, they crush. Everyone is terrified and superstitious. They're jumping at shadows. I watched them stone a man to death, then burn his corpse to ash outside the city—all because they thought he had the plague. Influenza, maybe, but not… not anything like what was seen during the Crisis. The weather has been horrible, too, so of course everyone is getting sick. It's that time of year."

The young woman dropped her head into her hands for a moment, trying to breathe and fight back tears.

"What of your father?" Grayden didn't ask, he just snapped up the lighter Sarah offered him, and lit up. Taking a long drag and letting the smoke trickle out through his nose, he glanced at Brynn. The prince had taken notice of the solemn look on Tylen's face—and the group gathering in general—and mouthed the word 'what?' Grayden shook his head at him to deter him, and the prince turned back to what Vix was showing him about knife angle—but the look he had given the archmage before he did so had been an eerie reflection of his father. It was also a promise that they would speak about the meeting he hadn't been invited to; and Grayden wasn't looking forward to that.

Rose coughed to clear her throat. In the end, there was no gentle way to put what she had to say, so she said it plainly. "My father is completely out of control, and the whole show is coming off the rails. If people weren't so afraid and beaten down, they would have done away with him already. Now it seems as if he has eyes on every corner—and a few unlikely allies."

"Such as?" Tylen asked, studying Rose so intensely that she fidgeted—which she wasn't normally prone to.

"A dragon. A young queen. I've not heard her name. She and my father speak often."

"What does she look like?" Tylen asked, his own tension visibly mounting.

"Pale hair and green eyes. She's like a ghost, thin and almost frail."

"Did your father call her by name?" Tylen asked, leaning closer. He could feel Grayden studying him.

"Luke? Something? They whisper most of the time. It was hard to make out from the secret passage to his offices."

"Lukka," Tylen said, two fingers coming to rest politely on Rose's knee—bringing her full attention to bear on him. She looked down at him, blinking in surprise. He rarely reached out to anyone except for Brynn. "Did you hear anything she said?" Gold eyes were like burning brands in the low light of the caves, intent on Rose, and only Rose.

"He wants the key."

"Isn't that what the rogues are looking for?" Sarah asked, her eyes meeting Grayden's for a mere fraction of a second before returning to Rose's.

"It is. I've been helping them," Rose said wearily. "I even know why they want it—and I think you do, too." The healer was looking at Grayden now.

The archmage bowed his head, staring down to the top of the table a brow arched wryly. They had him.

Somehow, he wasn't shocked; he only employed the best and the brightest. Shifting uncomfortably, he felt the damning weight of the piece of metal tucked into the breast pocket of his robes. "Is that what all of this is about now? A key?"

Rose turned slowly to look at Grayden. "It's about the cure. You know the golden rule: 'he who has the gold makes the rules'?"

"He who has the key, has the cure," The archmage took another drag off his cigarette, trying to bluff ignorance for as long as possible.

"That's what they want," Tylen said quietly. "The Angelic. They want the cure. The Baron thinks he can manipulate them and use them as a weapon to gain the power he seeks."

"No one can give my father the power he seeks," Rose said glumly. "A lot of people are going to die, and I don't think anything we do will prevent that. Even if it does go the way my father wants, we will have him to contend with instead of the Angels, and that... might be as bad, if not worse. As it stands, the Angelic don't have to lift a finger when we're killing each other."

The table had gone deathly silent, and no one wanted to make eye contact with each other anymore.

"Sonnovabitch," Sarah said flatly, brown eyes

widening as she stared down at the table—glancing up quickly to Brynn before looking away again. "I thought the key was just a damned legend."

"Legend or no," Grayden said drolly, "It seems that we've underestimated our enemies. I had no idea the filthy bastards could read."

Rose had noticed the way Grayden patted his breast pocket, and she and Sarah shared eye contact for a breath. Things… were about to get complicated. Sarah had said that Grayden was crazy like a fox, and that his actions since the fall of Skyeford had been purposefully erratic. Now, she knew why.

Chapter Ten

ynn leaned forward as the green dragon beneath
him touched down on the sandy limestone cliff.
Dust and debris were stirred up by her wings, and
he had to shut his eyes and focus on keeping his balance as
she backwinged her way down. He needn't have worried,
he knew she was strong, and he didn't affect her landing
that much; but he also didn't want to face her ire should she
decide that carrying him was a form of servitude—or worse
yet, ungratefulness. Thus, the sand hadn't settled before he
was scrambling down from her back.

Staggering, he realized his mistake too late, and
found himself murmuring a dizzy apology—then clutching
at her mane to keep his knees from buckling. His head was
still pounding, and his ears were ringing. Today had been
too much, and he was weaker for its events. It would have
served him right if his dragon companion had flown away
and left him to die; but she hadn't, and didn't seem inclined
to. Instead, she stayed still until he could steady himself.

It was only when he was able to bear his own

weight again that she settled onto her haunches; and as she looked on, he took the opportunity to shed his dripping traveling cloak. His shirt joined the pile a moment later, and then he set to work—studiously separated garments from one another and laying them out to dry.

Despite the flurry of action beside her, the queen's gaze drifted westward toward the Tel'av river. Around them, the sound of rasping grasshoppers was carried by updrafts, and occasionally, a falcon called as it circled—but other than that, everything was still and neither of them spoke.

The tan and craggy stone they were perched on was part of the range that sheltered Tel'aven, and it provided a natural buffer between Tel'dorath, the white city of the dragons, and the Exclusion Zone—the place the Angelic spacecraft had crash-landed. The Tel'av mountains also bordered a fertile tract of farmland that had been dubbed 'Cideshaa', which was where most of the Cideshii immigrants eked out a living. Tel'strathos and its most notable feature, Mount Athos, were located to the south; the great mountain rearing up past the tangled shield of the rainforests and foothills like a final warning to turn back.

From this height, it felt like Lynn could see forever—see everything—and he couldn't help reflecting on Draconic superstition surrounding Tel'strathos and its capitol city. Many dragons were so afraid they wouldn't even look in the direction of Sine… not that Lynn blamed them. The city had done awful things to humans and dragons alike—and the monarch had witnessed some of its horrors first hand. He also knew Grayden had been born in Tel'strathos, the years of his childhood spent at the base of the mountain in a sleepy farming village; so he harbored some mixed emotions.

"They are moving," the queen murmured into the silence, making Lynn jump. She had gone so preternaturally still that he had almost forgotten about her; but now that she was back with him again, there was something heartbreakingly human in the fluorescent gleam of her eyes. She was still staring westward in a way that unnerved him—and in the same way he doubted she wanted to look south, he didn't want to look toward the Exclusion zone in the west. He didn't want confirmation of what he already knew in his heart.

"Yes, Empress. They are." Lynn suspected she had been watching her borders from here for a long time, as there were grooves worn into the stone of the overlook that matched the size and spacing of her talons. She had been coming and going from this height for ages, and most like alone. So why had she brought him here? He admittedly felt like he was intruding.

"I seldom see them outside their broken craft. Today, they are about—and in broad daylight, no less."

"Is that what you were doing? Getting close enough that you could watch them?" Lynn asked. The highest point of a mountain range was no trouble to a dragon determined to assuage her curiosity.

"Wasn't that what you were doing down at the river?" she stated boldly; daring him to challenge her or make an excuse.

"I was running for my life," Lynn corrected guilelessly—and was rewarded with her acceptance as quickly as she had been willing to mistrust him.

"So it is true? They were chasing you? What do you have that they want so badly?" Her temper had cooled as suddenly as it had flared with her suspicion.

"You know that answer. It was your mother who gave the key into the keeping of my house."

At that, the queen's head swung around; regarding him coolly as she made a low hum of nervous concern. "So, it has come to this?"

"It is what they want, and what all of us want: health and freedom. What *won't* they give for that?"

"Why not give it to them?" the queen replied.

"I'm not so foolish as to think giving them what they want will end our problems, or theirs..." Lynn sat down exhaustedly, arms around his knees, dark back turned to the sun so his hair would dry. He would regret his choice later when his tresses became a nightmare he was unable to comb; but he wanted to be as dry as he could be before the sun set. Being soaked during a cold desert night was a death sentence.

He was lucky that he had been rescued, but he didn't intend to push said luck and assume his savior would stick around. His mount had run off with most of his survival gear, and his sword was gods knew where—probably on the bottom of the river. He had no water, no rations... nothing.

"Do you have it?"

Lynn thought about that loaded question carefully. "I do not—though it is with those I trust." He had been tempted to tell her it was in Jasper's saddle bags, but instinct told him to keep lying to a minimum when he was conversing with a dragon who—deep down—was spoiling for a fight.

The queen laughed at his reply—a low, rumbling growl that served as a Draconic equivalent to the human sound. "You tricked them."

"I'm leading them away from my family."

"And you led them here to mine." Her voice was sharp, but not with anger—it was fear.

"I don't mean to correct you, Empress, but as you've noted... they were already here."

He only got a sharp, high pitched snort of annoyance in reply.

"Where is your mate? Is he well?" Lynn asked, nudging a rock with the toe of his boot. The question was meant to be disarming, and he hoped it would comfort the queen. It seemed to have the opposite effect, though.

She rounded on him, turning only her head; giving the impression of a praying mantis about to snap up prey. "I need no mate to protect me."

Well. That had not gone as intended... "That's not what I meant. You had recently taken him as a mate when I was a boy. I was there with my mother for the ascension ceremony, as were many other dignitaries. I couldn't have been more than five summers. Your mother had just passed, and you were the first dragon I ever truly beheld. It might seem strange now that your kin have left Parliament, but I often wondered how you both were faring."

The queen's expression softened, the scales around lips and nostrils losing some of their tension. "It is as I thought. I do remember you." Tearing herself away from her self-imposed vigil, she rose to pad over to Lynn. Leaning down, she nosed at his shoulders and hair. She was scenting him again, this time more carefully.

"The first time I made your acquaintance, you were very small. Fresh from the egg."

Lynn didn't correct her—it was a Draconic figure of speech. "This is true," he said. Their first meeting had been much as their reunion—if less aggressive. She had been the first dragon he had ever been close enough to touch; and while his mother had introduced them, the empress had lowered her muzzle to breathe in his scent as all of the palace of Tel'dorath looked on. He had been so young, then, a toddler at best—but he remembered how in awe of her he had been. He still was, really. And she? She had been… so sad. Magical, beautiful, and full of grief.

His mother had later explained that her bonding ceremony had to happen much sooner than anticipated because the old empress had died unexpectedly. Now, as a man who had married, lived a life at court, raised a son, and buried a wife and newborn… he had a much better understanding of what she had gone through.

He also knew what the scars on her forelegs meant. He had not been the one to free the empress, she had escaped on her own—and he still felt guilt that he hadn't gone to help her sooner—but her subsequent withdrawal from Parliament had been what it took to galvanize those who were on the fence about the evil-doings of Sine. In a way, the liberation effort was the empress' doing, even if she had wanted no part of humanity's petty squabbles any longer.

Back then, Parliament, himself included, had lost sight of the big picture as they struggled to wrangle back freedom from the Guild Republic, and to overcome the last vestiges of a survival system rooted in slavery and oppression. He also suspected that was exactly why the empress was up on this rise—so she didn't.

When he felt something warm and wet hit the back of his hand, Lynn found himself looking up at the dragon with a new appreciation. Bright green eyes blinked away Draconic tears as she sorted through her own bevy of memories.

"I am sorry, for the loss of your kingdom." She said. "And for you. To one whom much is given, much is taken. Your heart is unwell, as anyone's would be, and so you have come home to the deserts and the rivers—to the cradle of human life, and the heart of magic. Perhaps it is not an end, but a beginning."

Lynn hadn't been expecting the show of empathy, and he found himself re-evaluating the being before him. She was fast becoming a person to him, a woman and despite his drive to free her kin, he hadn't connected with a dragon in such a way before. "Perhaps that is true," he said wearily. "And while I thank you, I should also be on my way. Did you see what direction my mount ran?" He was pushing, and the silence that followed his words let him know he had nudged a boundary. He wasn't exactly a hostage, but he didn't have time to waste, either.

"I do not know, mortal, if I can let you pass into my lands. I do not know if I can help you—if we… can help you. I do know your horse has run far. Perhaps the Angelic ate him, perhaps they did not."

"I'm truly sorry if I brought more trouble upon you, M'lady." Lynn's expression was cautious as he reached up toward her—but she pulled away before he could touch her; clicking her teeth at him as if scolding a rambunctious hatchling.

"It matters not. Where there are humans, there is trouble. That is the way of it—and to befriend your kin is for a dragon to accept suffering. But…" Derailing further attempts to apologize, she turned her scaly back to him as she shapeshifted into her human form.

Shaking his head to clear some of the arkane residue from his eyes, Lynn blinked at her as he took in the change—and she turned to give him a tight-lipped smile. Her human form was nothing less than stately. Her most striking characteristic was her long green hair, which was pulled up into an intricate braid that trailed over her shoulder. Elegant hair pins and scintillating chunks of alexandrite were plaited throughout it, and shining emerald disks decorated her ears. In contrast, a simple white silk blouse's yoked neck swooped along her pale collar bones, the fabric thin enough that it might have been revealing on anyone else. Her bare feet were like a pale, shimmering mirage against the tan sands, and her flowing green skirt trailed to the ground in gauzy folds; muslin and silk cascading over each other in alternating ripples. Simply put, she was as stunning as a human as she was a dragon. "But?" he prompted, feeling short of breath again.

She offered him her hand. "But you are here, and that is more than I can say for your Parliament. Walk with me?"

"Do I have a choice?"

"No."

Brynn had been curled up against Tylen's chest, sleeping soundly thanks to the potion that Rose had made for him; but now he was murmuring restlessly in his dreams, fingers twitching as if trying desperately to clutch onto something. With a gasp of the word 'no!' he startled awake in Tylen's arms, and the dragon followed him as he clawed his way upright.

Tylen needed less sleep than Brynn did—being Draconic had some perks—and he might have been guilty of lying awake studying the other boy, which he felt he could do for hours. This desire was far more potent when Brynn was sleeping and his face was peaceful, but he digressed. "Just a bad dream," he soothed awkwardly, patting Brynn's shoulder as the other boy looked furtively around the room.

The prince's quarters were private—a large space near the back of the caverns that now had a makeshift door made from binder twine and a hole-riddled saddle blanket—but they were far from soundproof. In the distance, the sleepy peeping of dragonlings could be heard, as could the hearty snoring of Copelan in the officer's quarters.

"What time is it?" Brynn asked disorientedly, loose hair frizzing around his shoulder like sea foam.

"Not a minute past midnight. You fell asleep at the fire, and Grayden carried you back here."

"Oh." Brynn pressed the heels of his hands into his eyes, wiping away sweat and tears.

"What did you dream?" Tylen plucked at the other boy's sleeve with the tip of a claw, the touch careful but persistent.

"I… I was falling." Brynn murmured from beneath

his hands. "I was climbing a mountain, and then I fell. Everyone I love was falling around me, falling past me, and I tried desperately to catch any of them, protect them, but I couldn't. It doesn't sound sensical when I'm awake, but when I was asleep..."

"When you were asleep it was terrifying and real. The way I understand it, human dreams are the way your minds make sense of what happens to you during the day."

"My poor brain must have a lot of things to tackle then," Brynn tried to smile in the low light, though if it was visible to Tylen it must have looked rueful at best. "Do dragons dream?"

"Of course we do! And, like humans, a lot of what we do is remember things. The way I understand it, a little more accurately, but it doesn't seem too much different. Do you want to try to go back to sleep?"

"I don't think I can. I need to get up," Brynn said. "I'm afraid the nightmare will pick right back up where it left off if I don't."

Sighing, Tylen nodded. Standing stiffly from the pallet on the floor, he offered the other boy a hand up. He then waited for Brynn to bind his chest—unobtrusively helping to hold wraps and readjust tunic before he took his hand again. Pushing aside the blanket blocking the door, the dragon couldn't help thinking what an unkempt sight they made; Tylen's hair barely bound in a sleep braid, and Brynn's loose and wavy like a lion's mane. Luckily that wasn't as much of a worry in the low light of the caves.

Every so many feet, arkane lanterns had been lit, and the dim glow gave the caverns a feeling of comfortable closeness that Tylen was beginning to find reassuring. Brynn, however? He couldn't speak for. He knew the prince was still shaken, and struggling to adjust to all the changes and loss.

Hand in hand the two made their way to the Great Hall—and true to form, mages and dragons were still awake playing chess. Some were curled up on bedrolls sleeping, but for the most part everyone there was still up. A good half of those present were part of the night strike team, and had grown used to midnight hours—and those that weren't watching or embroiled in the games were serving mugs of hot herbal tea and placing friendly wages. There was a level of peace to the caves at night that didn't exist during the day—and Tylen sometimes wished that humans were diurnal so he and Brynn could enjoy such times more often.

The young mage also realized he had been wrong about the direction of Copelan's snoring. The drake must have dragged himself to the main hall to have another nap, which explained why Tylen had heard him so clearly. He seemed to have only recently woken and was sitting next to Maylin, the two of them pressed close in their human forms.

The reason why they were awake? Tylen had his suspicions when he saw Maylin holding Freya's runty dragonling to one shoulder, rocking the hatchling as she fitfully protested her bedtime. The whole scene was painfully domestic, and it seemed to have given Brynn pause. Neither he nor Tylen had been noticed yet, and his grip tightened painfully on the dragon's hand. "What is it?" Tylen asked, whisper so low it was barely audible to Brynn.

"This is my fault."

"Your fault? This isn't perfection, but we are warm, and dry, and safe for the time being. This is the absolute best you can expect from a situation of this magnitude. You are a good prince, and will be a good king one day."

Brynn shuddered silently, the motion felt between he and Tylen's clasped hands—and the dragon pulled him closer. "Do you want to join them for chess?"

Brynn took a ragged breath, and this time it was loud enough to draw the attention of those by the fire. Copelan rose from where he sat when he realized who their visitors were, gesturing that Brynn should take his place; but Brynn's willpower crumbled in an instant beneath his guilt, and the prince just as quickly changed his mind.

Shaking his head politely, he let go of Tylen's hand and turned on his heel—walking quickly toward one of the adjoining tunnels leading to the officer's quarters.

To Grayden, it felt as if he had just managed to fall asleep when he was roused by the soft rap of knuckles on limestone. The sound was timid, and he knew without opening his eyes that Brynn was lurking in the doorway. Forcing himself upright, he reached out with his arkane abilities to light the lantern at the foot of his bed roll—and blinking in the sudden brightness, the archmage proved his own prophecy. Brynn was indeed there, and so was Tylen—there was no mistaking the golden glow of Draconic eyes. Grayden wanted to shout, he did. He was exhausted. But when Brynn strode across the room and sank down to curl up into the bedroll beside him, he swallowed every word on the tip of his tongue.

Tylen was much more timid, following only because Brynn had felt safe to do so; and as the prince made himself comfortable beneath Grayden's camp blanket, Tylen knelt beside him, gaze meeting the archmage's beseechingly. "He had a nightmare," the dragon said hesitantly—determined to avoid giving away a confidence, while conveying what he thought the other boy needed.

Grayden held back a smile despite himself. "So now that we're all here, what are we going to do?" Sleep was the obvious answer, but Brynn still had an aura of panic around him that was undeniable. The boy hadn't quite learned the Broderick trick for ignoring fear yet—for which Grayden might have been annoyed, but he was also grateful. Soon enough, time and the weight of leadership would harden Brynn's heart—so the archmage tried to celebrate the honesty while it lasted; or at the least, not punish it.

"I can't sleep. Don't make me, please? I'll lie here quietly. I..." Brynn halted himself before he started to plead. He knew he was acting childish, but whenever he'd had bad dreams, he had only ever found comfort curled up between his father and Grayden. He knew he was too old to be cowering in his stepfather's bed; but right now, he couldn't do this. He couldn't pretend he wasn't shaking. He loved Tylen, but he couldn't lose time with what little was left of his family, either. Not when Grayden was going away soon, and might never be coming back.

"So I gathered," Grayden answered mildly, biting his lip between sentences to remind himself not to yell. "You don't have to ask, I understand."

"I... I could tell a story if you both would like that? Just until Brynn feels tired?" Tylen was trying to rescue the situation as best he could, and the smile he offered Grayden in the lantern light was simultaneously hopeful, and sheepish.

"I take it you promised?" The archmage asked, the ghost of a smile lifting the corners of his mouth.

"I did," Tylen chuckled, seeing how tired and cranky Grayden was. For a man who didn't want to be a father, and certainly had his own issues, he attempted to be patient.

"This is on you, then," Grayden grumbled.

"I said I would. Don't you like stories, Archmage?"

"I..." Grayden looked down to where Brynn was curled up next to him, and stifled another longer sigh, "Do," he finished lamely. Stroking the prince's hair back gently, he then tucked the camp blanket tighter around him, and scooted over—allowing Brynn to lie between them, and invite Tylen onto the far side of the pallet. It was a tight fit, but it was doable.

Tylen still moved hesitantly, afraid to be struck for assuming to be allowed in the bed; but Brynn was there, and Grayden and Tylen had spent time in close quarters before with little to no incident. Thus, the dragon was eventually convinced to settle onto his side, leaning into Brynn protectively. The physical contact infused a calm into the situation that hadn't been there before, and Brynn's eyelids were already growing heavy at the familiar comfort of Grayden's presence.

Tylen's expression softened further at Brynn's response. In the dragon's mind, the archmage could argue all he wanted, but he was already a father—Tylen just wouldn't be the one to break it to him. "How about the story of the First Flight?" he suggested. "It's not a happy story, not exactly, but… maybe it will make you feel less alone?"

Brynn made a sleepy rumble of sound that translated roughly to 'okay' while Grayden remained strangely silent—so Tylen went ahead.

"There is something you need to see," the empress said.

As Lynn fell into step with her, he couldn't help his amazement at how tall she was in her human form. As a child, she had towered over him. Now they were on equal footing, and she could look him in the eye when many others could not.

Scooping his cloak and tunic up off the stone where they had dried, the king clutched them loosely as he followed the dragon across the plateau. He felt like he was forgetting something, and while he was definitely shirtless,

he couldn't help but think he was more or less...
completely naked. The desert was not a place to find
himself unprepared, and it added to his discomfort.

All he had was a survival knife. He had no food, no
water, and no supplies; and like her though he did, his
companion could well and truly kill him in a dozen
different ways if she was so inclined. It didn't help that her
every action seemed meant to remind him of that fact, and
it took all his willpower not to fidget.

The high plateau they had landed on had a carefully
hidden set of inlaid sandstone steps. Said steps were
unnervingly narrow, had no railing of any sort, and spiraled
up the rock face of the peak that continued up from the
plateau. A man looking skyward from below would never
have glimpsed them. Lynn's stomach tightened, and the
bottom of his feet started to sweat as he looked up. And up.
And up. He suspected that the second smaller plateau atop
the climb was their destination.

From what Lynn could tell, the staircase had been
carved by wanderers ages past, and then been worn
completely smooth by the elements. Human and dragon
feet had done the rest. It seemed a strangely popular place
to be, for something long forgotten—and ten minutes of the
most terror wracked climb of his life later.... he knew why.

He'd had to maneuver himself carefully up behind

the empress—the steps were so narrow there was scarcely room for the ball of the big man's foot—but when he finally arrived at the true peak of the spire, the view took his breath—and it had nothing to do with the altitude. It felt like he could see forever…several hundred miles of forever. It was the sort of place a man could be sure of the movement of many things, from herd animals to armies—which certainly explained its level of wear.

Far in the distance, over the fork in the river to the east, Tel'dorath still rose. The white limestone domes and pillars were ant sized and blinding in the sunlight. Naturally, they had been what he focused on first. Had he not known it was a city, he might have thought it a temple of some sort. A city built on a lake looked almost supernatural from great height—especially in a desert.

Around the glinting domes, blue, green, and brown veins of delta and marsh twisted, kissing the scintillating ribbon that the Tel'av river had become. Marshes and riverbanks made honeycomb patterns—much like a cleverly sewn quilt—and to the south there was a vast smear of multi-hued green that denoted a tangle of rainforests and jungles.

Thoughtfully, the king bit his lip. It was a shame that dragons never ventured south willingly, because the rainforests had some of the most unusual and beautiful creatures within them. So did the foothills of Mount Athos. Vile though Sine might have been as a capital city, there were some places of note within Tel'strathos.

"How did you find this?" he asked, still short of breath and finding words difficult. The air was thin at this elevation; and had the land not been so flat around them, the spire they had mounted would have been wreathed in clouds.

"Man built upon this place, but I have taken peace in visiting often. From here, I can see far. Very far. Legend has it that your kin believed they could communicate with the gods if they climbed this spire. I can fly up, but for them, it was a pilgrimage of sorts."

"I can see why." Lynn wiped his brow. "Is that why we didn't fly?" The king was hurting in places he didn't know he owned, and the climb up had reminded him that he was not as young as he used to be. It also might have proved that he wasn't as fond of heights as he was... tolerant.

"Walking is good sometimes. It reminds us to look up as well as down. It has also given me time to think about what I should do."

That answer didn't entirely please Lynn, but it was an answer. He was debating what to say, his gaze drawn back toward the domes of Tel'dorath—when he felt the dragon's hand come to rest on his shoulder, and she used her grip to turn him to the west. "There is much to see here. A goatherd can find the best pastures for his flock, and every oasis for miles. But it provides me with even more important information. There. Tell me what you see?" She pointed a claw-tipped forefinger.

Lynn squinted. To the west, Fort Drax rose. Wreathed in tall towers and brightly lit, it was one of the bigger forts in the area—which made it easiest to identify from a distance. Among the fort's ranks, Cideshii were the primary support. It was their way of lending to the safety of all who lived around the Exclusion Zone… but that wasn't what caught Lynn's eye.

"M'lady?" He breathed. "Is that what I think it is?"

She flashed him a canine punctuated smile, and when he looked back again at her request, he used his hand to shield his eyes. Squinting over the edge of the foothills peppering the border between the Exclusion Zone and Tel'aven, he knew what he was seeing—but it was getting his brain to process it that was the hard part.

Within the zone, there was motion. The sort of motion that was so big it was unmistakable. "They've fixed their ruddy ship, haven't they?" There was the white-violet glow of arkane repulsors flashing fitfully, and every so often, the faint creak of metal—audible all the way up where they stood.

"Almost," the empress said. "Soon."

"The moment they get the cure, they intend to leave?" Lynn intoned, trying not to sound hopeful.

For lack of a better description, the Exclusion Zone always looked… surprised—and that was fair, as most of its geological damage had been done by a crashing spaceship. The twisted wreckage of metal lay in a deep crater, and the stones around it shimmered with contamination as they writhed away from the point of impact. Nothing that went into that area came back out, at least to Lynn's knowledge, and that was why the zone around the ship had been labeled as forbidden to all peoples.

Then there was the unlucky bonus of the alien species of plants and fungus that now thrived in the area— presumably having arrived on the hull of the Angelic's ship. Some of that non-native flora had taken root enthusiastically, and it glowed red, purple, and green in the day's fading light—enormous mushrooms and gas pods marching steadily toward the border of Tel'aven and beyond. The Angelic might have been reluctant to leave their ship, but their invasion continued biologically—a thing Lynn doubted was entirely accidental. "I'm grateful my father didn't live to see this day," he whispered.

"I would say the same for many. Some days I wonder why I brought my children into this world. A world that does not feel like our home anymore." The empress' green eyes were fixed on the Angelic spaceship as it fitfully rocked in its crater. It was so very far away—and entirely too close. "I fear that even if they do get the cure they seek, they will not leave us in peace. I think they will destroy us all before moving on to enslave another world."

Lynn nodded, still staring because there was little else he could do. The Exclusion Zone was far more alien than any other place on Anteas. The crash site had become twisted and polluted—heavy metals and radiation had gushed from the engine cores that drove the spaceship. The only clean part of Angelic technology were the bits that ran on the arkane... but how they—a people who couldn't wield the ability as it was lethal to them—managed to harness it was beyond him. There were theories, however. Dark theories...

"Have you had any mages go missing of late?" the empress asked. It wasn't so much a question as it was a statement—and the way their trains of thought aligned made Lynn aware he wasn't the first to consider what he had.

"I feel sick," Lynn replied, looking away and crouching as he tried to catch his breath. He wasn't entirely certain he was done vomiting from drinking most of the Tel'av, but that wasn't what was making his knees weak. It wasn't his pounding head, or the ache in every part of his body. It wasn't the burns, or the tickle in his lungs, or the stinging in his eyes—it was what he had seen in Sine, and what Grayden's fate could be.

"Child of the desert..."

"Empress?" Lynn couldn't look up. He was pridefully refusing to be sick, but he was hovering on the edge.

"Lenna," she corrected. "I have a name, I am not my crown."

"Now where have I heard that before?" Lynn chuckled—then closed his mouth before he regretted opening it.

"From what I understand, stubbornness is a trait you and I share, King Broderick."

The dragon knelt beside him, taking his face into her hands. He didn't fight her, but he couldn't meet her eyes, either. "Lynn. Just... Lynn."

Her thumbs stroked his high cheekbones, a warm-cool tingle following in their wake. There was a glow building around her as flowing blue-green wisps of magic roiled from her fingertips... and it felt good. His heart skipped a beat. He had heard of dragon magic, and how it could differ from the more common human expressions of the arkane. He had heard that curative magic could be a powerful force of healing or harm, depending on the dragon's will. Right now, he hoped Lenna's will was good, because if he was wrong, he was already dead where he knelt.

"What are you going to do. What are you thinking?" The empress' tone was sharp, the amount of concentration she was expending on Lynn making her words harsher than she intended them to be.

"I want to know where Grayden is," Lynn replied hoarsely. His nausea was easing, and the pain in his eyes had faded to a dull ache. She was healing him, and that was… extraordinary. He had heard that some ancient dragons remembered the way… but humanity had destroyed them first in their desperation for a cure. They should have been extinct—and their knowledge with them.

"You wonder about the fate of your mate?" Lenna's hands became gentler still, and there was sympathy in her posture that was matronly. "I do not blame you. I wonder after mine as well."

"Has he gone missing?" Lynn asked, giving himself points for still being able to hold a conversation despite the bizarre sensations he was experiencing.

"Not missing, but he has not been my mate for a

very long time. Sometimes I think he is already dead and gone—the dragon I fell in love with has changed beyond recognition."

"Is that why you're out here so often?" Lynn thought back to the claw marks in the rock face—marks that had become grooves.

"I don't want to go home. And I don't know what to do. This world makes no sense to one such as me. Not anymore. Everything has changed, and I do not know if I truly have a home to return to."

As the pain eased in his chest and back—the burns along his arms and cheeks finally closing—Lynn cast his eyes down, nodding into her touch. "I'm afraid it doesn't make sense to me anymore, either." The magic, though? That was something incredible. For a mortal, Lynn had lived a full life; he had seen Grayden's power and nearly every other sort of magic under the sun, but this—Lenna's abilities bordered on miraculous, and that gave him a badly needed burst of hope.

His concerns about the empress and her relationship with her mate... that was a different story altogether.

Chapter Eleven

Brynn nuzzled into Grayden's shoulder, blue eyes dark with worry and red-rimmed with sleeplessness. Against the prince's side, Tylen curled up tightly. The dragon was watching both of his companions, and when they finally appeared settled, he lifted his hand, fingertip trailing the space above him. Their attention was on him, and he decided to show them something they had likely never seen before. It was a risk to offer Draconic knowledge to mortals, but he felt it was worth it. Whatever he shared with Grayden and Brynn wouldn't be disrespected, and it might even help foster deference between their peoples.

"A long time ago, before the Crisis. Before the Old World—there was the First World. In the First World, there was no moon in the sky, and the nights were dark." Moving his finger through the air like a paintbrush, a warm blue-green glow filled the room—and slowly, an image shimmered to life at his bidding. A planet vastly different from the state of their own was lost in shadow beneath a dark sky, and the stars were the only thing punching holes through the blackness.

Tylen heard Brynn take in a breath of surprise, his eyes flying to the dragon's face before returning raptly to the wavering image.

Grayden looked equally enthralled before he reached up, trailing his hand curiously through the picture—sending it rippling wildly before it solidified again.

"Neat trick, Kid."

"It isn't a trick, it's my memory. It's flight memory," Tylen said softly.

"I've heard of this magic, but I've never seen it used. I thought it was dead. There are only a few dragons alive that are powerful enough to control this sort of thing..." the archmage trailed off, looking at Tylen with a new sort of respect—and suspicion.

"Grayden," Brynn said, voice rough and hushed. "He's telling a story. I want to hear." The 'be quiet' was heavily implied.

At that, the archmage gave a chastised chuckle—still not able to tear his gaze away. "It's like a cellular memory, or racial memory?"

"Both," Tylen said, his voice deepening with concentration as the inky shape of dragons in flight blocked out the stars. "The world was dark in many places, and giant beasts roamed the earth, just as dragons did. Mankind? He was merely a wraith in the shadows. It was the time of dragons."

Within the shimmering patch, a flying dragon landed—its scales glittering in starlight before it dissolved away somewhere near Tylen's ring finger.

"The gods decided that the world was too dark, that too many powerful things roamed. There was no balance, and there were too many great beasts. So instead of deciding who would live and who would die, they presented magic to the greatest and the least upon the face of the planet. Dragons, and mankind." Within the shimmering shapes hovering above then, a prehistoric looking human reared up and took shape, holding an arkane torch. The flame glowed violet as the human swung it like a bat, his image disappearing in a wild flaming arc that left Brynn and Grayden blinking.

"Dragons were careful with their gift, while humans were reckless. Dragons use their powers to heal, to create—from the bones of the first dragon to die a mortal death, the great city of Tel'dorath rose. The city of my birth..." Tylen's voice broke, and he felt tears threatening. There were times he was so homesick it hurt.

In the vision above, a blazing sun rose over a

brilliant white city, dragons of every color circling it.

"There was day and night, a set cycle. Dragons were born, and the birds and beasts grew plentiful; but then mankind made a terrible mistake."

A crimson gout of flame filled the scene, an enormous ball of fire descending toward the white city.

"Fearful of the remaining night, and the cycle of life and light, human mages tried to summon a sun that would never set. And a great meteor fell from the heavens. The gods wept."

For an instant, there were corpses everywhere within the glowing shimmer above Tylen's hand. Everything went red, and there was a tangle of beasts, men, and dragon corpses. Death. It was all death—and Brynn took in a sharp breath.

"In compassion, our empress wept tears of blood, for she and so few of her kin had survived. As those tears fell upon the earth, the gods heard her sorrow. From the still body of her mate, the gods made the moon you see hanging in the sky today—to comfort her grief, and to remind humans to never be so afraid of darkness that they committed future atrocities."

The corpse of a bloodied silver dragon rose limply in the sky amidst the shimmering magic field, growing ever larger and brighter until he became the moon in the sky.

Around him silvery meteors fell upon the earth—and kneeling in the shattered streets of Tel'dorath, the empress lay weeping, her pale white robes stained in the multi-hued lifeblood of her kin.

"The empress grieved, but her heart did not turn to war. No. She vowed to only use her powers to heal from that day forward. She swore to teach her children control and respect, and to watch after humans least they forget. But humans? They were stunted by the dread of death and their short lives. They forbade magic, and killed anyone they could find who had the gift—dragons included. Humanity's fear, it twisted them, and that is when the first world became the old one."

There was one more glimmer of magic before the picture faded, the last scene one of the empress reaching up beseechingly to the light of the moon... before fading away completely.

Tylen lowered his hand. He could feel the pain and palpable shock of the two men beside him. "I know it isn't a happy story, but it is a true story. It reminds me that bad things happen, and even when I am sad or hurt, that I should still have faith in the good in the world. And in man.

"What happened to her... to them?" Brynn asked hoarsely, clinging tighter to Grayden as he stared up at the cave ceiling above them, seemingly disappointed that the image had disappeared.

"She raised her children, and then she flew away one day—on the day when the moon is closest to Anteas. She flew until she could go no higher, and she was never seen again. It was believed the gods took pity on her, and she was finally reunited with her mate after all their lonely years apart."

"Oh," Brynn said thickly.

"So it may be a painful past, but it is not without hope. From the empress and her mate... all dragons are descended. We are tasked as stewards of magic, and of history—ours and man's—and despite all the things that have gone badly, that magic has survived. We have not failed, and we are not without hope..." Tylen didn't sound completely sure, but he was trying.

Brynn eased an arm around Grayden's waist as he felt his eyes closing against his will. He was excited by the beauty of the magic he had witnessed—and saddened by the story that Tylen had to tell. It wasn't devoid of hope, Tylen was right, but the fact that Brynn could relate more than he wished was overwhelming.

"Get some sleep," Grayden said—his voice thick with what sounded suspiciously like unshed tears. He patted Brynn's forearm as he let him snuggle into his chest... and he didn't complain when Tylen's arm overlapped his, the dragon bracketing the prince between them.

"Tell me magic isn't dead for humans, or dragons. That we haven't broken everything? Lie to me if you have to…" Brynn's voice cracked as he trailed off into the quiet.

"I assure you that it *is* not, *has* not, and *will* not." Grayden said resolutely. "Tell me, Brynn—when you watch the aurora on cold winter nights, or when you see a beautiful bird or beast, does it still take your breath? Do you still feel wonder?"

Brynn nodded. "Yes, the first time I saw Tylen I felt that way. Or when I found myself alone on the snowy plains between Skyeford and Belden… I could feel how vast everything was, and how small I was, and that didn't scare me, it felt incredible."

Grayden could sense Tylen's eyes on him, and he couldn't help smiling through his own grief and exhaustion. "Then the dragons did their job. Magic is still alive, and some humans remember how important it is. You can't extinguish magic, because you can't kill hope."

The room was silent after that, Brynn dropping off soon after the archmage stopped speaking—but Tylen and Grayden were sleepless long after, and kept a silent watch together; one that was filled with a mixture of optimism and fear.

Grayden rose far earlier than he needed to, tucking both sleeping boys back under the blankets. Almost instantly they coiled closer to each other, seeking warmth in the chill radiating from the cave stone; and he smiled. He needed time to think, and to put himself together.

Tiptoeing out of his quarters, he dodged guards, drowsy officers, and sleeping dragons to let himself out into the morning light. Peering up, he considered the weather as he bit his lip; watching fleecy clouds threatening to overwhelm the sunrise with a blanket of gray. There would be more rain today. It wouldn't be a bad time to travel as their tracks would be muddied and their scents washed away, but he didn't favor being soaked for the umpteenth time. It felt like he hadn't been properly warm or dry for any length of time in months.

In his pocket, he felt the weight of the key, and he tugged it from beneath his outer robes—holding it in the palm of his hand reminded him of its emotional and physical heft. Regarding the dark fabric wrapping, he found it ironic that something so important was so small. He could take the damned thing with him, and probably should, but that was also the worst decision he could make right now.

If Lynn was still alive, he had led the Angelic away to protect his son, his kingdom, and the key; his sacrifices would be in vain if it fell into enemy hands. If Grayden gave the key to Brynn now, the boy would become a target—but that would only come to pass if someone figured out Grayden didn't have the damned thing anymore; and he planned to make that exceptionally difficult for their enemies to ascertain. If it was his turn to play decoy, he would do it right.

Lighting a cigarette, the archmage leaned back against the tree roots that made a convenient seat outside the cave mouth. He was tired, and he was ever so slowly beginning to admit the strain of leadership and warfare. Maybe, just maybe... when Tylen was of age, he would step down. Retire. Maybe he and Lynn could steal some time together that wasn't punctuated by extended absences and political red tape.

It was as he took another drag that he felt something bump into his boot. Going perfectly still, he waited patiently, and soon enough he was rewarded with the scrabbling of claws ascending his trouser leg—and a curious snout poking its way over the top of his knee. "Hello, what have we here?" Grayden lifted his leg to examine his new... attachment, and had to stifle a sigh. Dragonlings weren't anywhere near developed, just as human infants weren't—but they were equally as sensitive, if not more so, to emotion and tone. They also developed more quickly, which meant that by the time they had reached their first year, they were as intelligent as a seven or eight year old human. It was around that age that they would shapeshift to their human form for the first time; but until then, they were stuck in dragon form. "Well?" he asked, taking another drag and setting his boot down harder than necessary.

A trilling peep was the only response he got as his leg was scaled again—Freya's wayward multi-colored dragonling insinuating itself into his lap thereafter. Grayden was tempted to shoo it off, to tell it cigarettes were bad for babies; but it was already happily trilling and clambering up his robes to nudge into the gap of his tunic, searching his empty pocket by sticking it's head inside… then following the scent of the key to his hand. "That's not for you…"—He held the beast away from him for a moment to check gender. Male dragonlings had a bump under their scales that a female did not—"Little girl," he finished sternly. "No. Not for you at all."

He put the key back into his pocket and tightened his robes again, settling them neatly under his utility belt, and received an argumentative squawk for his troubles. "I have to give that to Brynn today. Don't tell him if you know what it is. Just help keep an eye on him, okay?"

The dragonling gave him a burbling chirp in response, finally moving to sit on his knee and stare up at him intently, chest puffed out and tail twitching—looking more like a house cat than a dragon.

"You know we will," a woman's voice interrupted.

Grayden turned in surprise, finding himself staring at Freya in her human form. She was tall, olive skinned, and had stunning sienna eyes.

"I'm sorry if she's pestering you. She likes you. You were the first face she saw when she hatched, so..."

"Tell me she didn't imprint on me?" Grayden worried.

"Maybe she did, maybe she didn't. But she certainly likes you."

The dragonling had only managed to be a good soldier for so long—and had moved to chewing on the top tongue of Grayden's right boot. His robes had parted as he sat, and the exposed leather looked like a nice place for a baby dragon to teethe. "A little young for a jailbreak."

"Being the last to hatch proves her the most willful of my brood. I thought she might not survive, but as you can see, she is happy enough now."

"Freya, if I may..." Grayden reached down to remove the dragonling before she could reach flesh with her teeth. She ripped away from the fabric with a screech of protest before he placed her back into her mother's arms, and then moved over to make room for the queen to sit.

She did, the dragonling burrowing into the front of her tunic—taking the hint that now was not the time for play. "What is it?" she asked gently.

Grayden fought down the urge to pull away, to change his mind. He wasn't good with feelings. He most certainly wasn't good at talking about them—let alone to dragons—but he couldn't burden Brynn or Tylen, and he still had to find a way to tell them about the key without making things worse.

"I don't know what to do," he admitted. "I don't think I'm special in that regard but..."

"You worry for the children. Are you planning to return?" Freya asked.

"You recently lost your mate, this isn't fair to you," Grayden said. "I wanted to tell you that I'm sorry. And that the Fifth is family, and we take care of our own. If there is any way that I can help you..."

Freya reached over with the hand that wasn't holding the dragonling, placing two long, claw-tipped fingers across the top of Grayden's. "Don't be sorry," she said softly. "You had no more control over what happened than my mate did. Time and again you have protected your soldiers. My mate… he knew what he was doing, and what he was signing up for. You freed him, you and your king, and he died fighting for a world where no dragon would be chained or tortured again. You gave everything, Grayden. Your family, your life, your name… yes I know of the brand and what it means for men like you. Now you've lost your kingdom, and for what? Helping us. For fighting against those who abuse their power. It is I who should be telling *you* that I am sorry."

Grayden slowly turned his hand over, taking those two fingers and clasping them sorrowfully. They were warm, and felt very human.

"I will watch over your young drakes, Archmage. We all will. We aren't here because we have no other choice. We are here at the caves because when we are together, we are free. We are Skyeford. And so are you."

"This is for you," Grayden said, placing the cloth bag into Brynn's free hand.

"We walked all the way out here for this?" Brynn asked.

"I would have flown us, Archmage," Tylen elaborated, sounding almost insulted. "You need only have asked."

Standing in the middle of a cold forest, seemingly alone, and huddled around a fallen tree—Grayden, Tylen, and Brynn had taken time to speak privately. It was barely eight in the morning, and the prince was still clutching a dented tin cup in the other hand—it was full of hot coffee, which he wasn't drinking so much as using to warm his hands.

"This is important. This... is the most important thing in the world right now. Worth more than your life, Brynn, or mine. Worth more than all of Skyeford and possibly most of Anteas," Grayden murmured.

"What is it?" Brynn asked, turning the bag over thoughtfully with his thumb.

Tylen was standing so close he was all but in the prince's pocket—curious about how something so small could be *that* important, while simultaneously filled with a vague sense of terrible *knowing*.

"A key," Grayden said.

Tylen's eyes were fixed on Grayden now—so serious they could have bored holes through him. "What sort of key, Archmage?"

"The sort of key, Master Dragon, that everyone is looking so hard for."

"A key? That everyone is looking for?" Brynn was confused, and he set down his coffee cup on a nearby tree stump so he could have a better look at what he held.

"How long have you had it?" Tylen asked, tone suspicious. He was remembering the impromptu meeting around the rickety, makeshift table… and the strange moment of fidgeting when Grayden had patted the breast of his robes—right where undertunic pocket would have been. Tylen *knew* now. He was certain. Grayden had been hiding the thing away the whole damned time, and he probably hadn't told a soul until now. The young mage's Draconic sense of honor was deeply injured, and his temper rose sharply until he checked it—if only for Brynn's sake.

Brynn, however, was ignoring the tension and the shift of emotion from Tylen; and when he didn't get an immediate answer from either mage, he started to loosen the bag's drawstring.

"It was given to me by High Commander Jensen. King Broderick handed it off to him before he rode out to look for me," Grayden replied to the dragon, sensing his upset—and finding it telling.

"King Broderick knew… this, all of this…. would happen?" Tylen asked in disbelief. Did everyone know except for he and Brynn?

"Knew and responded according—Brynn!" Grayden reprimanded.

Struggling the pouch open at last, the prince had

dumped a smooth piece of rectangular metal onto his palm—then froze mid-inspection at Grayden's parental tone. The key, if it was a key, didn't look like any sort that Brynn knew. It... was flat. Along the edges there were raised bumps and grooves, and down one side there was a smooth filmy stripe. Strange writing chased itself along the unstriped edge—etched in a language that Brynn had only seen once or twice from the old world. He couldn't read it, but some scholars still remembered. "It doesn't look like much, does it?" Brynn said.

"You put that back in its pouch or so help me..." Grayden swiped the key from Brynn's hand bad-temperedly. "Seriously. Don't touch old world technology. It'll make you stupid. Or Sterile. Or both."

Brynn let Grayden take the key back from nerveless fingers.

"He's exaggerating," Tylen interjected. "It's been next to his heart for weeks. If it was going to harm you now, the Archmage would already be dead and we wouldn't be having this talk."

"Or sterile," Grayden grumbled. "Don't forget that one."

"This is... I haven't had this much cheer in a conversation since last Yule," Brynn said facetiously, watching Grayden re-wrap the bag. "Would someone tell me why this key is so damned important?"

Tylen narrowed his eyes at Grayden. "You do it, or I will," the dragon hissed. He wasn't pleased about being left out of the loop on something that could be considered a Draconic matter… and finding out Brynn had been deceived, too—it didn't make him happy. So many lives had been lost for something so small!

Grayden took a deep breath in through his nose—tucked the pouch briskly into the top of Brynn's chest bindings without an iota of remorse for the invasion of personal space—then let the breath out. "Right." He coughed, clearing his throat.

"Please, Grayden, tell me what you've been keeping from me for weeks. I'd love to hear all about it," Brynn said, hand coming to his hip defiantly—unknowingly the spitting image of his father.

Tylen's glare went from expectant to outright silently demanding.

"I'm working on it, Tylen. Prince Broderick, keep your trousers on. There has been no coronation and I still outrank you. At least let an old man get his bearings before you start throwing your weight around."

The dragon raised an eyebrow.

Grayden rolled his eyes. Children were so serious nowadays. "You see, a long time ago there was a plague that killed off most of the human population. Some people were immune. Those people turned out to be dragons and Half-dragons. Old world scientists made a cure from Half-dragon blood. They also made a vaccine. Every human who is alive today is here thanks to their ancestors getting that vaccine. Immunity is passed down through generations of descendants; it altered the recipients DNA to make it impossible for them to contract the disease."

Brynn's mouth was hanging open, and he hadn't closed it yet; so Grayden took the opportunity to continue while he had the proverbial floor; shock and awe campaigns were a tactic he was finding more and more useful in his old age. Tylen, however, looked less surprised, and more incensed—then again, a dragon would be. Tylen grew up with knowledge of the Crisis as fact. Brynn had been sheltered. Even Lynn had, in a way. Grayden had been trying to carry that burden alone, but now he saw it had done no favors for anyone. "The Crisis was a terrible low point for humanity, and knowledge of the cure was locked away for safe keeping as soon as scientists were sure that the virus wouldn't mutate," he continued. "Besides, the world as everyone knew it had been destroyed, and people were desperate to rebuild and put the past behind them. Your great-grandfather was tasked with keeping the key you now hold, Brynn. He gave it to the dragons in a time of greater peace. The dragons, in a show of good will when they were allowed a seat in Parliament, gave that key back to your grandfather—who gave it to your father before the Baron had him assassinated."

Brynn's eyes were huge. "I never knew who… go on…"

"The Angelic are here because they have the same disease that we are all immune to; they caught it from us, and they want a cure. They want that key, Brynn." Grayden stopped there, letting what he had to say sink in as he reached for a cigarette.

"So everyone knew about the key except for me, and I'm the one Father chose to have you hand it off to? What about Tylen, he… he's a dragon. He must have grown up hearing this story. I… never did." Brynn looked suddenly overwhelmed, tears filling his eyes, but not spilling. "You must think I'm stupid. And maybe… Maybe I am. I must be. Ignorance is bliss, right?"

Grayden hadn't expected this turn of events, but he was certainly in trouble with Tylen. The dragon shot him a dirty look before turning to take Brynn's shaking hands in his.

"Brynn… Prince Broderick, nobody thinks you're stupid. Not all dragons know about the key. In fact, only a few of us do. No one is having a laugh at you. Your father probably didn't want to burden you, and besides, if you don't know, it's less likely you'll be tortured and killed. It kept you safe..." Tylen was trying to deescalate the situation as best he could—and he could read by the expression on Grayden's face that it was the wrong move long before the prince's temper snapped.

The archmage was rubbing his temple, head bowed, when Brynn finally rounded on Tylen, pulling his hands from the dragon's grasp.

"Safe like my people? They didn't know, and look how *safe* it kept them?!" Brynn gestured back toward the way the three of them had come—toward the Foothill Caves. "Tell that to all the dragons who lost their lives, and their grieving mates. Tell that to all the fatherless children, and mothers who won't hold their babies tonight!"

Unknowingly, the prince had grazed the root of Grayden's silent guilt, the casket in which all his ghosts resided, and the archmage stepped back like he had been struck—even though it was Tylen who was taking the brunt of Brynn's grief, embarrassment, and outrage.

Sitting mechanically on the tree stump, Grayden took another drag of his cigarette, then picked up Brynn's cooling cup of coffee, taking a convulsive swallow. If he had his mouth full, he wouldn't be tempted to open it. He refused to let Brynn know his words had struck home. The prince really was like his father. Lynn, too, had a knack for finding just the right buttons to press for maximum damage.

Tylen observed the way Grayden sat down, and his confusion only grew; especially since he hadn't meant to upset Brynn—but the prince was clearly directing hostility toward them both. The dragon fluttered uncertainly in place for a moment, fingers flexing where he had been forced to let go of Brynn's hands. Silently, Tylen tried to decide on a course of action—and finally, he reached out; patting the back of Brynn's hand with two outstretched fingers, expression wounded. The motion was one that mated dragons might share, asking for elaboration and understanding.

The gesture was so confused and pleading that Brynn was eventually able to curb his temper. He didn't understand the Draconic gesture—although he recognized it as something he had seen between Maylin and Copelan more than once. What Brynn was deadly certain of was that his anger was getting the best of him. He took a deep breath, held it for a count of ten, and then apologized. "I'm sorry," he said levelly, wiping away his tears with the edge of his sleeve.

"Apology accepted," Grayden muttered into his stolen coffee.

It was only then that Brynn realized he had hurt Grayden, too. Swallowing hard, the boy put his emotions back into place, and taking Tylen's hand in his again, he stepped up to hug the archmage—the gesture sideways and awkward. It was met by a gentle pat to the arm from Grayden, who leaned away long enough to exhale a lungful of smoke.

"I'm really sorry."

"You will be. I just finished your coffee." Grayden didn't let the hurt reach his eyes—he never let his enemies see him bleed; and most certainly not his friends and family.

"Are we… is there anything else I need to know?" Brynn asked flatly, trying to remedy the situation he had created.

Grayden turned his head to stared at Tylen levelly; his opinions on the dragon and his mysterious child-soldier origins clicking into place in a manner that was tempting to confirm. 'Need to know' indeed. It was tempting to tell Brynn to direct that question toward Tylen; instead he let it go. A man had to keep secrets at times—and for a dragon make that double. It was how the world worked. "I don't have anything more to tell you, no. But you may find one or two people around you that have a lot more to say than you first realized."

Grayden made eye contact with Tylen, letting the dragon know he wasn't fooled. Tylen looked away quickly, hand squeezing Brynn's convulsively. Luckily, the prince was still too upset about everything else to catch the background drama. Grayden did know Tylen's flight. He might even have been able to make a guess at parentage. Scratch that, he did know; and Brynn would either be elated, or scandalized…

Life was always so chock-full of interesting twists and turns.

Brynn held the dragonling to his shoulder. She had escaped to join him while he saw the rescue party off, and he was glad for her company. The squadron might have been an elite military force—but everyone who was part of it looked nervous in their own way, which was perfectly fair. Most that journeyed to the Walled City never came home again.

At least Ella appeared as cool and collected as she always did. Vix seemed believably jittery, and Donovan? The rogue looked well pleased. Whatever he was so smug about, Brynn was certain that it wasn't good; but it also reminded him of a piece of scuttlebutt he had heard today.

Vix and Maylin had allegedly engaged in a public

heart to heart about what it meant to be a dragon—or a Half-dragon. Mind, Brynn had already heard previous rumor about Vix—and how he might have survived the grievous nature of his wounds—but he wouldn't have guessed the gunner was a dragon. Half-dragon. Whatever. The concept of Half-dragons was something Brynn made a mental note to privately speak with Tylen about. He felt like he was missing a great deal of information, and if he was going to lead, he needed to know.

Beside Brynn, Tylen rested a hand unobtrusively at the small of the prince's back. He was at eye level with the dragonling, who gave a shriek of concern as Grayden shouldered his pack and settled onto the back of a hearty looking bronze drake. Said drake was one of Grayden's first recruits back in the days of the Liberation, or so Tylen gathered from the chatter around him.

The handful of men and women that were accompanying the mission looked relieved to finally be doing something; and Tylen could agree with that drive. Part of him still wished he was going with the rescue party; but then he turned to watch Brynn, really watch him, and he knew he was needed here. "All will be well, My Prince," he whispered near the exhausted human's ear. "He will return to you. He made a promise."

"What are we going to do?" Brynn murmured as

Grayden gave everyone a last cheerful wave, stubbed his cigarette out on his boot heel, and tightened down the saddle strap the bronze had been fitted with for travel. The rest of the Archmage's team mounted up not long after, readying themselves for the upcoming flight.

"We take care of everyone until Grayden comes home, we keep... things safe until your father returns. It's what we have to do."

Brynn gave Tylen a slight nod, grateful for his warm touch at his back. The prince's heart was lurching, and he wanted to beg Grayden not to go. Part of him couldn't shake the fear that this might be the final time he saw the other man—and that the last thing he had done was rail at him about doing the best he knew how, in a situation that he couldn't control. "Do you think he knows I didn't mean what I said?"

"He knows," Tylen said. "I'm a dragon, and I know he knows. Things will work out, My Prince. Have faith. Promises mean a great deal from some men—especially men like him."

Chapter Twelve

hey had been flying for some time when the empress started to circle. They hadn't reached Tel'dorath yet, so Lynn couldn't help but wonder what they were searching for. Beneath him, wildebeest and antelope raced away from the dragon's shadow. There was a grumble of thunder to the east, tall white clouds spiking into anvil shapes as the horizon darkened, and the king felt the first drop of rain hit his arm. The rains were coming, and flying would be impossible until they passed. "What are we doing?!" He called as they lost altitude, Lenna drifting like a weighty and serene kite toward the cracked earth beneath them.

"I need more time," she replied, landing smoothly and effortlessly.

Lynn clutched her neck spines, his balance much better now that he wasn't stiff and in pain. He had to admit he felt more like himself than he had in days. There was still a tingle to his body that reminded him strange magic had mended his wounds. It wasn't unpleasant or distracting, though, it was more like a low level hum. "You aren't concerned about the storm?" he asked, sliding off her back to land in a crouch.

As he straightened, her horned head tilted and he found himself being scrutinized by one intense green eye.

"I fear no storm."

"Are you leaving me here, then?" he asked.

"I should, for your own good." The dragon became human, then, leaving a roil of arkane dust shimmering in the Tel'aven sun.

Lynn could never get over how incredible it was to watch a dragon shapeshift. "For my own good? Empress, I am a child of the desert. I know my way here as surely as I did the halls of my keep in Skyeford—but this far from the river, and close to your home. I could be killed by a stray drake who thinks I have trespassed, and if one of your kin doesn't, the sun will for certain."

"It might be better that way," Lenna said blankly, her head bowed so that Lynn could not see her face behind the fall of her hair.

The king read the fear and frustration in her posture. Why would she rescue him only to abandon him now? She did not strike him as cruel… "M'lady, are you afraid?" He reached out to her carefully; but before he could touch her elbow, she turned on him fiercely.

"Do not assume to touch me—to comfort me! You cannot right this! No man can!"

Lynn pulled his hand back, but he didn't move away; stubbornly refusing to bow down to her fear. If he could shoulder it for them both, he would. "Empress..."

"King Broderick!" Her accented voice was sharp with wounded pride, as she drew herself up to her full height.

"I'm sorry," Lynn said gently, resting two fingers on her forearm—touching cautiously, and in a manner he hoped she couldn't misinterpret. As the two of them stood frozen beneath the gathering storm, he couldn't help noticing the way his dark skin contrasted with hers—as stark as the differences between their peoples—but his touch was respectful, and he suspected that was why she didn't pull away.

When her gaze finally met his, there was so much despair in her that it took his breath; and as the rain began to patter down around them, she bowed her head—her tears joining the parched earth at her feet. "He will kill you. I cannot go back. You cannot go back. What do I do? Everything has changed, everything is broken!"

It was dawning on Lynn that this was the first time she'd had an equal she could speak to; and he could see how much the burden she carried had been weighing on her. "Your mate?" he asked softly, opening his arms moments before she threw hers around him, burying her face into the crook of his neck. She was trembling so hard it made his heart ache. Pulling her closer to him, he tucked her taller frame under his chin to shield her from the rain and steady her. She smelled of jasmine—and the warm earth around them meeting the cool rain was equally as fragrant.

"I don't know him anymore," she whispered, her full lips brushing Lynn's skin as she spoke. Around them, the tap of rain became a hissing roar, and the desert took her first breath in months—a sort of magical shockwave that could only be experienced in person, not described. "I do not even recognize my kin. My children are gone, I know not where! All is lost..." her voice broke in her grief.

The lash of the downpour reached a crescendo, lightning skipping from cloud to cloud above them. "Do you want my help? What little a man such as I can offer?" Lynn asked, voice nearly lost in the furor of the storm.

"Help us. Help me. I cannot put this right..."

Grayden tried to stretch his bad leg as subtly as possible. Tabris was a big drake and it wouldn't disrupt his ability to fly, but the archmage did try his best to be a courteous passenger. They had skirted the edge of Gent proper, choosing to fly along the shore of the bay rather than take their chances with any stray Angelic or artillery that the Baron might have lying around. If the intelligence Rose had provided was accurate, Belden and Gent were hotbeds Grayden didn't want to touch his toe to, let alone immerse himself in.

To make matters worse, the rain hadn't let up—but as uncomfortable as being drenched was, it was nothing like the terror of the most recent snow storm. Grayden was glad to see the backside of winter, and he reminded himself of that amidst the cold, thin air. He felt Tabris' worried rumble, and reached down to pat the bronze dragon's neck to silently reassure him. A few more hours of flying, and they would all be able to rest.

Just as the archmage managed to find a more comfortable position, a gust of turbulence hit them from the east, and he found himself scrambling to keep his balance. The jostling pushed his hood down, and as he tried to guide it back up over his head, his gaze was drawn beyond the cloud cover. If he concentrated, he could see the cape of Gent. There was a small space of open water between the tip of the continent and the large island that lurked off the coast of the land mass.

Lost Island, or Wandering Island, was a place that

was inhabited by the peoples of Xastin. If Grayden had been so inclined, he could fly south of the island until he reached Hastos Village—the place he had been banned from the local bar. He wasn't, though, and they would be bearing easterly soon. Flying into the wind would be difficult for dragons and passengers alike, but it was necessary to reach the shores of Cideshaa. There, his company could stop and regroup.

It didn't seem like it would be soon enough, though. He had his concerns for everyone's health and well-being. Vix and Donovan were sharing a ride, so they would at least stay warmer doubled up. Ella and the rest of the mages who had accompanied him would be less lucky, and he had to keep that in mind.

Brynn was sleeping off the stress of the day. Hardly ten minutes after Grayden had departed the caverns, Sarah and Rose had sought the prince out and sat him down to discuss the details of leadership—who would hunt, who would search for healing herbs to make the medicines that might be needed, and who would see to water and sanitation. Then Sarah and Brynn had exchanged notes on what was expected by Grayden. The caverns were a place for refugees, but Helith housed a fully functioning military division. Skirmishes were to be had, and Brynn had nervously agreed to keep watch over rotation. It meant he would be going back and forth between camps often, as often as Grayden had, and Tylen was to be at his side—which was no hardship for the drake, as that was where he desired to be.

They were back in Helith now, and after the emotion of seeing Grayden off and shouldering his new position, Brynn had fallen deeply asleep. Tylen couldn't help feeling relief that they were within the rebuilt fortress. The Foothill Caves felt more like home, but Helith was a safer place for a prince—even if the location served as a decoy in case of emergency. It sounded harsh, but a rag-tag group of civilians would never be able to protect the Crown the way trained, battle hardened soldiers could. It still wasn't perfectly safe in Helith, but it was easier to sleep knowing someone was always on watch.

That said, there was another reason it was good to be back. Brynn had his own room in Helith—a *real* room that had become he and Tylen's—and the dragon was grateful for the privacy on more than one level. Not only did it allow him time to speak with Brynn and focus on the relationship budding between them, it also gave him space to sort out everything else. As the wayward son of the Empress of Tel'dorath, he found himself involved in more than one delicate situation... frequently.

When Tylen had left home, his parents had been so embroiled in their fractured relationship they had hardly noticed his absence—or been grateful for it, considering the day he had refused his right to ascend. His mother had been urging his kin to withdraw completely from the fate of humanity, while his father had howled for blood. As the debates grew longer and tenser, his sister Lukka had become stranger and stranger—she'd always been more twisted and dangerous when left to her own devices—and soon she had thrown her lot into the familial divide. She had chosen their father's side, while Tylen had taken no one's... though if he could have, the mage would have supported his mother.

Tylen also held deepening suspicions that his father was assisting, if not outright leading, the Separatist group—while Baron Forscyth was funding it. Tylen couldn't prove it, but Lukka's increasingly aggressive behavior was telling. She had moved beyond playing devil's advocate to outright sycophantry. She'd always had warped views of who Tylen was, and her desire for him to mate with her was not a new issue.

It was true that once, long ago, the way that an emperor or empress gained their power within the flight was to marry a sibling. It was thought that such actions kept the royal bloodlines true—and since dragons were genetically diverse, it was rare that offspring would be negatively impacted. Tylen's grandmother and mother, however, had moved away from such thinking, believing the strength of the Draconic was in their diversity—and honoring that.

But being different, being gifted? That was what had killed Tylen's brother. It hadn't protected any dragon from human greed and fear. The night Tylen fled had been the eighth anniversary of Rayen's death. It had been the night he was to accept his right of succession. He hadn't, and their father had finally rounded on him in front of the rest of their flight for his disobedience.

His mother had been too shocked to step in—to Tylen, it had seemed she had abandoned him to their father's rages. He also believed that she was angry with him for refusing to accept his birthright—a thing which she had sacrificed much for him to keep.

The night hadn't gotten any better for his parents, either. Tylen's sister had declined to ascend as well—though she had only done so because she didn't want to seem as eager for power as she was—and to curry Tylen's favor. Said favor didn't last long once her solution to his refusal was proposed. She had effectively convinced their father that she would be a good mate for her brother, and that a physical union would cement Tylen's position until he came to heel.

Tylen's mother only wanted the safety and happiness of her people. In her book, that meant leaving humans to their own business—which was less extreme, although incongruent with the First Empress' vision for her people—but his father? Tyraen wanted blood. His rage at what had happened to his mate and son had taken over. He once would have given anything for his family, but what he saw in his forays into Sine had broken something inside of him—and Tylen had often been the target of his frustration, especially when the younger drake wouldn't agree to acts of cruelty.

After fleeing, Tylen had often wondered what had driven him to fly toward the rainforests—toward the taboo land of Sine and all the evil therein. He knew the truth now, and could admit it to himself. He had wanted revenge. He had wanted to hate humans. He had wanted to destroy humanity for what they had taken from him and his family, and the way they had mutilated his mother. Instead, through his capture and the horrors he faced, he had developed compassion. Silently, he thanked the humans he had met— and the dragons who had yet to escape a society where their only worth lay in what could be taken from them. They were the reason he was here with Brynn now, and why he had lied to join the military. It had seemed to be the only way he could really make a difference—and now he would be damned if he abandoned Anteas. It hurt to think of his mother and her pain. It scared him to imagine her alone with the monster that grief had made of his father; but those were things he couldn't help—Brynn, he could, and through him, Skyeford.

Tylen still feared what would happen when Brynn found out what he was hiding. The prince thought his partner to be a simple dragon—another young man like himself. When he discovered that Tylen was the heir to the empire of Tel'dorath… would it break his trust? Would it be construed as a bid for power, and break *them* before they even had a chance to be? Part of Tylen wanted to blurt the truth out now—before the beast could became too big to slay. But how could he explain any of this? Where would he start?

There was one more secret, and it was, technically, the biggest one of all. Brynn already knew it, he only had to connect the dots. It was the reason that Rayen had multi-colored scales, and was the reason that Tylen's kin had been given the key to begin with. If the Draconic empire knew that their empress carried human blood, they might revolt against her—which was another understandable reason to be terrified. It was her side, her mother's line that was to blame. New life had been created out of love, but dragons could be amazingly stuck in their ways at times—and as big and important of a step as an interspecies union was, it was still considered traitorous by many dragons.

Tylen didn't know what to do, so he watched Brynn sleep—the way his fingertips twitched as he dreamed, and the cupid's bow of his full lips moving in silent words. He was perfect, and precious, and his life was worth fighting for as much as any dragon's. Tylen simply had no idea how he could fix what had come to pass. But there had to be a way... and Brynn held the key.

Brynn sat primly at the table, but the way he held the cup of hot tea in his hand was anything but formal. He was still exhausted, and had wanted to keep sleeping. Instead, he was sitting across from Miles, Tylen at his side, and they were discussing war. More than war, really—they were chasing a past that had become elusive at best. "Commander, I need to know," the prince said softly.

Miles raked his fingers through his silvering hair, expression conflicted. "Brynn, your father wanted to protect you. He did his best to let you be a child for as long as possible. So did Grayden, for that matter. But that time has come to an end. As you might have noticed, it is both a point of great pride, and sorrow. It's part of growing up, and I know you need that truth now—but I also don't like being the one to break this to you. The task should fall to your father."

"Who told him?" Brynn asked, voice so small it was almost a whisper.

"I did," Miles said wearily.

"Twice in one lifetime. That's heavy work," Brynn replied, gaze still fixed on the swirling tea in his cup, brows raising in empathy that he didn't know any other way to express.

"But you need to know."

"I do."

"Then I will tell you."

Outside the window, the watch was changing, the makeshift barracks at Helith already running like a well-oiled machine. *Once a soldier, always a soldier*, Brynn mused. "You know who killed my grandfather, don't you? It starts there. I heard mother and father talking about it on more than one occasion."

"The Baron had him murdered. It was the Cideshii who stepped in at that time. Forscyth had been hoping to pick his horse in the race. What he hadn't been counting on, was Galta."

"Galta?" Brynn knew the Cideshii in question.

"The Baron had a candidate in mind, one that he hoped would take the reins until your father could be crowned. A candidate that he could later influence your father with. Mind, his first idea was to slay Lynn as well—that would have gone better for him. Unfortunately for the Baron, your father was away in Tel'aven with your grandmother at the time, and the culling passed him over. Your grandfather also knew what was coming, and before Lynn left, he gave him the key."

"The Baron didn't want to tip his hand, so he hid behind false good will for my father. He hoped the candidate he pushed would heavily influence, if not override father in Parliament. Am I correct?"

"That's right. But it didn't go his way. He didn't understand how the Cideshii Hives work. Galta is a higher caste in his Hive, so he took your grandfather's place in Parliament until your father's return—which we almost couldn't convince him of, by the way."

"I bet Forscyth was furious."

"The Baron was positively seething, and he slunk back into the shadows to lick his wounds when your father was crowned. Oh, he tried to discredit your family, Brynn. Your mother, your father. He even started a rumor about Draconic blood in the Crown line, hoping that the dragons would leave Parliament."

"Would they really have done that, even if I do have Draconic blood somewhere?" Brynn asked, tilting his head toward Tylen.

"Yes," Tylen answered carefully, trying to keep his expression neutral. He didn't want to draw attention to what he was hiding, but he didn't want to lie, either. "The lineage of our royal family was very... selective," Tylen answered. "There was a time being Half-dragon was considered worse than death. Even *we* can be prejudiced. Sometimes dragons are worse to other dragons than humans are."

"I see," Brynn said. "This is because of the Crisis?" He was careful to keep his voice low, as he heard footfalls in the hall.

"Yes," Tylen answered honestly. "Humans have been horrible to dragons since the dawn of time. They called us monsters and demons while they venerated the Angelic. They were ignorant and cruel, and they murdered us and tried to drive all magic from us—and their world. Then, when they were unsuccessful, their excuse was that they wanted something from us, so they suffered our presence. They killed us, they tortured us, they enslaved us in the military and dissected us in labs in the name of finding a cure. In the end, it was the 'filthy half-bloods' that had what humanity needed—and there was resentment among my kin. Humans who mated with dragons were traitors, and vice a versa. Many half-bloods felt like they had no place, so they joined the military; some in hope of not being forced to conscript, some in the name of fostering peace, and rarer yet—were those who hoped to find a home."

"What about you?" Brynn asked when Tylen finally trailed off.

Tylen didn't flinch, and he thought quickly. "I... can't go home, My Prince."

"But why? Because you have human blood?"

Tylen winced, then nodded. It was a wound to his pride, but if Brynn wanted to focus on that, it was the most logical explanation for the time being. Perhaps he would be satisfied with that, and not ask how Tylen knew what he did.

"Can any of this be salvaged?" Brynn asked. "Can having this... key really change any of this? If I somehow find a way to put this right and there turns out to be a completely ideal outcome with the Angelic—what guarantee do I have this won't all happen again?"

"It's a good question," Miles said. "And I have an answer for you that isn't an answer. Do you want to hear it?"

Brynn eventually nodded, taking a long swallow of

his tea, expression far away.

"I used to think that we needed to abolish Parliament. That Skyeford should be its own entity again, as it once was before your father's father. But I know now that won't work. All governments, especially monarchies, have a chance for corruption. You have heard it from Tylen himself: even dragons are fallible. So, I supposed the question is: if you are just going to go to bed again in a few hours, should you make the bed? What's the point, am I right?"

Brynn blinked. "If all types of government become corrupt at one point or another, what's the difference between outright anarchy and our Parliament?"

"That's the root of the question, yes," Miles said, studying Tylen shrewdly. Just as Brynn had his tells, Miles remembered a dragon much like Tylen. One who had a golden mate. He had his suspicions of who Tylen was and why he was here. The high commander doubted a lot of things.

Had Tylen come to Skyeford out of rebellion? Necessity? Or was there some darker motive at work? The commander didn't think he had mistaken the situation. Tylen's love for Brynn was undeniable. But would the young dragon turn on them when they least expected it? If Miles said nothing and Tylen was a Separatist, Skyeford ran the risk of losing Brynn. If Miles tried to stand between Tylen and Brynn, he would lose both boys for certain. It could also come to pass that Tylen and Brynn encouraged one another—growing together as partners and men. They could be the best thing to happen to Anteas in ages, and if Miles interfered it could cut that off at the knees. So, the way he figured it, he would have to hope for the best and plan for the worst. Sometimes it was wiser to do nothing, even if it was the more difficult option.

"We have to do better," Brynn said after much deliberation. "We can't sit on our hands and hope that things will mend on their own—we have to *make* them right. Humans, Dragons, Cideshii… none of us can change what has happened in the past, but we can change what we do right now. Maybe that means that tomorrow will be a better place. It will never be a perfect world that we live in, peace is only temporary; but if we learn, we listen, and we try, our situation can certainly be better than this…"

"Why, Prince Broderick, I do believe you understand," Miles said warmly, his heart lifting. "There's more of your mother in you than you realize."

Chapter Thirteen

alta could taste Thaxl's anxious pheromones before he even brushed eye stalks with him. He radiated fear, and it was catching. Admittedly, their meeting held a clandestine note, but the time and place was not that suspect—then again, going out at all had become so, regardless of race or hierarchy. Thanks to the Baron's betrayal, the Angelic were turning Gent and Belden inside out unchallenged; and to say that they were destructive as they searched was a drastic understatement. Galta vowed they would never find what they were looking for if it was the last thing he did; he and the Rogue Queen had agreed on that much.

"How did you travel?" he finally asked Thaxl, looking nervously around the Dark Water Inn—one of Belden's finer establishments for visiting dignitaries. The Baron's clout had gotten the diplomat safely here, and Galta fully planned to take advantage of that windfall to meet with an ally.

Thaxl, the ever resilient envoy, had retreated to

Belden after seeing King Broderick safely off to Tel'aven—for which Galta owed him a dozen lifetimes of repayment. They both were lucky to be here, and thankful for Drishk's sacrifice. The noble Cideshii's death had allowed them to continue in the Baron's good graces—while undermining the terrible plans he had set in motion. Mind, Galta had no doubts that Forscyth was still suspicious of him—and hopefully him alone—but the man's repulsion toward his kin usually won the diplomat enough space to do as he pleased.

Waving a partially severed forelimb, the other scarred Cideshii offered the insect equivalent to a shrug. "It was as it is." The response was a deliberate understatement, meant to indicate hardship without acting like personal suffering was significant or unanticipated—an expected response from a hive worker.

"How fares Xastin?" Galta encouraged, trying to ask a more leading question without making the other insect too anxious to properly reply.

"Taos is concerned, as she should be." Thaxl clicked his mandibles uncertainly. "The Academy will lean whatever direction she takes, I think."

"They do not like to be involved," Galta hissed out wearily. "Was she truly here?"

"Before the time of the burning. She sent a

238

messenger to meet me here after Skyeford's ashes had cooled, and I told what I knew. It was a risk, but the message was not intercepted."

Taos was the leader of Xastin, a shogun. She was the firstborn of the Hastos clan, and was nearly ninety human years in age. Still, she was as fit and as healthy as any young human had been—which had led to rumors about a font of eternal life at her disposal. That, or Draconic blood in her veins, which was more likely than not. She had also never produced an heir, which concerned her country greatly; but that was neither here nor there.

"Her words were wise ones—though not meant for my tympanum, I think," Thaxl said, his eye stalks flushing. He was unused to so much attention, and it showed.

"That is good. Do they know the king lives?" Galta encouraged, needing to hear it again himself. The remaining loyalists required all the help they could get with Lynn out of the picture. Support from Xastin and the Academy could be a tipping point in taking back Parliament for the free peoples. Galta couldn't liberate or repair Skyeford, or put Parliament back together again, but he could round up those who were capable. It was now down to the matter of convincing them to cast their lots...

"The Crown is secure, or was last I laid eyes on him," Thaxl said, rubbing two good forefeet together like a fly who had tasted something delicious on the breeze. "His son survives as well, though few have seen or heard from either of them since the burning."

The uncomfortable grooming that Thaxl was taking part in spoke volumes of his fear and strain. To a human eye, it would seem a mundane motion. To Galta it was telling. Thaxl had been as disheartened by the fall of Skyeford as their human allies had been, and Galta didn't lack empathy. Thus, the pheromones inundating the air were finally too much for him, and his answering fear overflowed into an accented lisp, "I am sssorry, it is much to asssk of you, to take the place of Drissshk." Galta said.

Realizing how much his words betrayed, he then attempted to rein himself back in. He had to calm down. A small slip was not that terrible, not when he was safe in Thaxl's company—anywhere else, a show of anxiety could be a fatal tell. One never knew who was loyal to whom, especially right now.

"Drishk is still with us, in you, Hive Mind. But... is it too much to ask for peace? We left our overcrowded world for this one—the welcome was not warm, but we were allowed to stay. Can we not have our lives?" Thaxl nibbled nervously at the severed stump of his amputated limb.

It had never regrown properly, not in years, and at

this point Galta feared it never would. Their people were stressed—too busy struggling to survive for something as simple as a proper molt. "We owe what we have to Skyeford, Thaxl, lest you forget."

"I have not," Thaxl clicked. "And to tell you of what I know? Taos will return when the time is good. She has said so. For now, Xastin stays distant. Not out of faithlessness, but the Shogun will not throw away lives."

"That is fair. That has been the response of most of those loyal in Parliament. Ambis and Tel'dorath have ignored my requests for intervention as they usually do— just as they have the Baron's." Galta's expression was strained, his eye stalks quivering with his frustration.

"We are split, Hive Mind. In all things we should be one, but…" Thaxl made a miserable sound.

Thaxl was right, and so was Taos. Galta hated it, but it was true. He could throw his weight around all he wanted but it would do him no good until someone stood up to lead—which he could not do for fear of betraying those true to freedom. Half of his kin were Separatists, and they followed the Baron—the man who let Angels roam the streets, rotting and unchecked. There was no doubt in his mind what that meant was coming, and anyone with a mind of their own would see it, too.

But fear, fear was more contagious than any plague,

and it was alive and well between himself and his kin. Their world needed heroes, seen and unseen. Strength without faith was not enough. Not in times like this. Galta fluttered his wings. "We can do nothing until the Crown has returned, and that is the way of it. I know that East Harbor and Sine will rise to his aid, then." Without Lynn, many were powerless. The man had a way about him that pushed back the darkness.

"But will it be too late? The Baron has sold us already. Do you think Hive, divided as it is, can still stop this? Stop him?" Thaxl looked almost hopeful for a moment.

"We must step in. We must stand up. Like it or not, this is where our ancestors chose to be, and we must keep our promises. It is our land, too—even if its inhabitants do not think we belong. Enough of our kin have given our bodies to nourish this new soil… have we not bought our right to existence with blood?" Galta's expression was resolute., and Thaxl's pheromones soon changed to follow suit.

Lukka slipped wraith-like between the ancient hardwoods outside Helith, melting in and out of the shadows that the tall trees cast in the dying light. Her green eyes were fixed on the outer wall's side portcullis, and she was waiting. She had memorized when the guard changed, and so far she had not been spotted—this was all too easy. Being scented wasn't a concern as the reek of dragon was all over the place, she had many places to hide; as long as she didn't raise a ruckus no one would know her from any other mage… so she merely had to bide her time and wait for someone to get sloppy at the wall.

Walls wouldn't stop someone like Lukka, especially in her Draconic form; but luckily for the soldiers of Helith, she wasn't there to exterminate them. She only wanted one thing. Well, technically two. She wanted the key back, and the power that came with it—and her brother, and the power that came with him. Not necessarily in that order. Her brother *with* the key? Well that would be like a gift from the First Flight. It could happen, too, if she played her cards right—and Lukka was very, *very*, good at cards.

She also wasn't the only one who wanted the key, and that was why she was being so persistent. Just a few hours ago, she had diverted a rogue at the Foothill Caves. He went by the name of Donovan, if she recalled correctly—and he had been hoping to overhear the meeting between Prince Broderick and Skyeford's high archmage. She had made certain he hadn't; leading him in gratuitous circles until he was forced to admit defeat and slink back to the caverns, while she got a front row seat for what her brother and his allies were up to.

Their father wouldn't be pleased with what she'd overheard, and she would have a lot of work to do if Tylen wouldn't see things her way. Of course, she needed to catch him alone to do that, and of late he was joined at the hip with his pet prince. She couldn't even keep track of how many times she had been back and forth between Helith and the caves—keeping tabs on their blossoming relationship.

Briefly, the dragon allowed herself to enjoy her imagination—and what it would be like to shout Tylen's secrets from the rooftops. Tylendros. Son of Tyraen. Son of Lenna. Heir to the Empire of Tel'dorath. Steward of Tel'aven. A dragon, in love with a human. Pitiful, was what it was.

Cideshaa was spread out beneath Tabris' wings, and the low walls dividing plots of land looked like stitching on an earth colored quilt. Quaint, mud-brick huts and straw roofs stood out starkly from the snow-patched hills, and here and there the dull glint of sky in runoff water bonded the earth to the heavens. Sometimes the company would fly low enough that Grayden would catch a flash of bronze scales, or the flutter of his sodden, rust colored robes mirrored in the melt—but those moments were few and far between.

When the company wasn't avoiding vicious cross winds and turbulence by skimming the ground, they were fighting the cloud cover for visibility. Dragon eyes were built to handle the hazards of flying, but Grayden's weren't—which meant he spent a good portion of the flight with his face hidden.

Which was fine, as before they had hit land, he'd been having to reminding himself to breathe. He might have been an archmage, but he was uncomfortable flying over vast stretches of water. Boats made him even more nervous, so flying was preferable—but he still wasn't happy about the day's journey. Thankfully, they were closing in on the main city of Cideshaa—unimaginatively named Market Crossing—which was perfect timing. Grayden had gone from wanting to stop for the day, to *needing* to.

His bad leg was aching, and his hands had cramped into cold fists around handfuls of Tabris' bronze mane. Silently, he prayed that when he dismounted he wouldn't rip chunks of the thick, feathery stuff out. Dragons weren't fond of mane pulling, even if in a fight it was exactly what they used to protect the spineless portions of their neck.

"Here!" Grayden called over the wind, raising one arm weakly, hand still clenched into a fist. It would be enough to call a halt, and he heard a rumbling hum of affirmation travel through the dragons flying behind them. Everyone was eager to dry off, and the Cideshii within the city would be more than glad to open their homes to help. Any agrarian family was on Skyeford's side, as most of their trading had occurred within her razed walls.

The farmers of Cideshaa were as devastated by what had happened as Skyeford's citizens. They had lost those who supported their admission to Anteas and Parliament—as well as the influx of monetary gains that had once supported their Hives. Separatists would have been rather unwelcome; and by unwelcome, Grayden meant they would have been killed and buried in a back field, no one sparing them the honor of consuming their bodies—so it was fair to say that the fear of Separatist attack was as far from the archmage's mind as it could be.

"Here, here, here!" Grayden repeated, then gestured downward and out to the side where Tabris could see him wave and point. They would need space to land, and for Cideshii to gather. There was no way to make their entrance subtle—flights of dragons with mages riding them weren't a common sight—so the fields outside the city would have to do. It was determining which field was the right one that required experience. Luckily, Grayden knew more about farming than he'd like to discuss.

One tract of land was green with winter wheat, the tendrils poking through the last of the snow, so they wouldn't use that spot. The area Grayden was eyeing looked to be fallow—thus would serve their purposes while not destroying valuable crops. It was a small gesture, but it would endear them among the farmers. Courtesy. It wasn't so common anymore.

Brynn had retired early, and Tylen had gone with him. The two were now more or less always in each other's company, and the young dragon found himself treasuring any time they spent together; but what he loved the most was the quiet moments when they could say anything without interruption. Or more aptly, Tylen listened and Brynn talked.

The other boy was clever, kind, and always saw both sides of the coin. Tylen was in awe of that. Dragons could be so very black and white with emotions and logic; and exploring all the gradients of feeling and thought more empathetically... it was as fascinating as Brynn himself.

Tylen had started noticing the little things about Brynn—small things that felt like big things. There was something alluring about the way his unruly brown hair framed his face when not tied back, and the depth of his dimples when he smiled—the true smile that he only seemed to offer Tylen. Even the way he hovered in doorways while chewing on his lip—as if about to join in on a conversation, then never did—was charming. When they were around others in public, Brynn would speak only sparingly. Alone, it seemed, he had much more to talk about… and specifically to Tylen.

But what was most interesting to the young drake, was the motivation behind the other boy's behaviors. Unlike most humans, Brynn's hesitancy didn't indicate that he was shy or reserved; he was reading the room like an open book, believing that actions spoke louder than words. More fascinating yet was that when he was silent—he wasn't thinking about what he wanted to say to the exclusion of empathy as most tended to. He was genuinely listening; not to respond, but to understand. Tylen thought that was what he loved about Brynn most of all; and unlike how he judged himself, he could say without reservation that the prince would be an excellent king someday.

Which was why the dragon was torn about what he planned to do—arguing with himself internally while perched beside the bed. Brynn had dropped off almost immediately, exhausted by the day's events; but he wouldn't sleep deeply enough to dream until Tylen curled up beside him and let him press his knees into the small of his back. His full lips were parted innocently, his trust complete... and Tylen couldn't help but feel that faith was misplaced.

Once Brynn found out what he was hiding, he would most likely never speak to him again. There was deception in omission... and that would make what Tylen had to do even worse. "Why do you trust me? How can you?" he whispered the words, his hands shaking where they brushed a stubborn strand of hair away from the bridge of Brynn's freckled nose. "My father is your enemy... it might even be his fault you have no home..."

Brynn hummed in his sleep, stretching effortlessly before rolling toward the wall, and Tylen's heart hurt. Why couldn't he trust Brynn? Why couldn't he talk this over with him, tell him the truth, and ask him what to do—and if necessary, beg him to face this with him. They were... they were friends, and more, weren't they? He reached out two fingers, almost following through on his first reflex to wake the other boy. Talk. They should talk... His hand hesitated, then fell short, claw-tipped fingers splaying in the sheets where Brynn's warmth still lingered.

"Once I do this... I don't think I can fix this, or us, Brynn. I don't think you'll understand, and I know... I know what I'm doing is wrong. But so many people are going to die if I don't. My people, too. Yours… it's already too late for." The dragon wiped a tear away from his cheek by shrugging into the shoulder of his tunic. "I'm so sorry. I don't know the right way to do this. Maybe there isn't one."

Brynn was snoring softly now—more deep breathing than anything else—and Tylen squeezed the hand on the bed into a fist, his stomach clenching as if preparing to take a punch. "I'm so sorry." Steeling himself, the mage reached beneath the covers and into the other boy's tunic pocket, rummaging until he could feel the body-warmed rectangle of the key—resting right next to Brynn's steadily beating heart.

As respectfully as he could, Tylen lifted the piece of metal away, palming it before pulling the blankets up around Brynn's shoulders. For a moment he had felt the curve of an unbound breast, and it made him swallow hard. "I love you. Let me do this. I want to protect you. It should be me. This was my family's key first, so I'm just borrowing it back."

Brynn slept on, unresponsive, and Tylen knew he was trying to justify his actions to himself. He was afraid, and he'd seen too many bad things happen. An outsider would say that that it was selfish to make up Brynn's mind for him, but the prince had been through enough already.

"Sorry," he whispered again, then stuffed a travel pack into the place he would normally sleep on the bed. When Brynn woke at dawn, Tylen would be long gone; and before any more lives were lost, the Angelic would have their key.

Tiptoeing to the door, the dragon paused with his hand on the makeshift latch. He smelled something familiar and disconcerting from the hall. It was something Brynn couldn't sense, but a dragon could. It smelled of home, desert sands, and salt flats—and was nothing like the pungent smoke of wood fires, the crisp, nose-stinging sharpness of winter snow, or the earthy tang of thawing mud. There was only one person Tylen could think of who might smell that way; and his blood ran cold.

"Lukka," he murmured, letting himself out into the hallway while making certain the door latched noiselessly behind him. There were no guards at their posts, they must have been doing their rounds—so he would have to solve this problem on his own. Going as still as he could, he counted heartbeats while reaching out with every sense he owned—when from the corner of his eye, he swore he saw a flash of glowing green, and the glint of silver scales. Perhaps he was jumping at shadows, but he knew better.

How she'd gotten into the fort without being noticed was irrelevant… she was *here*.

Lynn sat inside the limestone cave, watching the rain fall. The desert was giving way—breaking up into rivulets of silver and muddy brown. It was beautiful, and destructive, and passionate… this making and unmaking of the land. Scorpions clung together to keep from drowning, and nests of ants floated by, legs hooked to make boats for their queen. Frogs and toads were rising from the churned and sticky mud, blinking awake after their long hibernation, filling the land with song in preparation for new life.

The rains had come! Soon the papyrus would bloom, spicy, green, and fruity—all manners of desert flora would be so thick and frantically prosperous that one could be overwhelmed by the fecundity. And here Lynn was, lost in thought with the dragon empress—contemplating ends not beginnings.

"I hated that we buried her in Skyeford," Lynn said softly, knowing that the dragon would understand what he was talking about. He could feel her curious eyes on him; and while she was shrewd and cautious, she was also not completely closed off from the world around her. She couldn't afford to be ignorant. Not in her position. "I wanted her to feel the rains, wherever she has gone."

"Back to the stars, where all the children of the

desert go. Why do you think dragons are so fond of watching the night skies?" Lenna's voice was reverent. She had known Aya well, and the two had kept company with each other when Lynn was not even thought of yet.

"Do you think she can forgive me?"

"You humans are made up of star dust. You are magic given flesh. Do you think a small matter like where she is buried will stop the star in her from finding its way back into the universe?"

Lynn smiled at that. "Nothing much stopped her in life. In death? Even less. Do you think she can see this mess we're in now?" He turned to take in the empress' green eyes. Wet emerald hair clung to her high cheekbones, and he swore for a moment he was young again, and the world still held some good. She was ageless magic, and his heart lifted for a few beats.

"What?" she asked him lightly.

"Nothing, I'm sorry," Lynn said, turning away again. "When I look into your eyes, I feel like she's still here. It's selfish, but I need that right now."

"Do not feel badly, not about that," the empress murmured, her voice husky with words withheld. "The needing of things, I mean. When I look at you, I remember the way it used to be. The way it used to feel when I believed in love. You have a way about you, Lynn

Broderick."

"I suppose that makes us even?" Lynn gave her a wide smile—a bright but empty thing in the shadows of the cave, and marred by the ghosts in his eyes.

"Perhaps."

"Perhaps. So, pray tell, while we're discussing what we don't know… what are we going to do? Me and you?" Lynn's expression was serene in a way that only a monarch who was practiced at deception could be.

"I don't know. But we have until the rain lessens to decide."

Lenna looked as conflicted as Lynn felt, and that was reassuring in a way he couldn't put into words. "Good enough. But what are you going to do while we wait?" 'Think' was the obvious answer, but Lynn didn't believe thinking could save them anymore.

"I am going to sit here," she said, folding her legs properly, her long, flowing skirt trailing across the sandy stone, "And I am going to wonder what it would feel like to kiss you. I won't, but it has been an age since I felt like I was alive. Would it be light? Soft like the rain on my upturned face? Or would it be heavy and passionate like storm clouds and lightning."

She gave Lynn an unabashed smile—the most animated she had been since they had begun talking—and for the first time, he felt like he was seeing the real woman beneath the facade. A dragon, but a woman all the same. "If it is just a kiss you want, Empress, I would risk it. My mate would understand, and yours will wish me dead anyway. I will warn you, though, it could become an international incident if anyone saw us." He gave her a warm smile, feeling her coming to life just like the desert—and he couldn't help but think how lucky her mate truly was… if only he could wake up from his anger.

"I said I wouldn't do it. I am allowed to think about something and not do it!" she teased, some of the stiffness leaving her posture as she brushed his clothed calf with her bare toes.

"A woman's prerogative. But remember this—some night when your heart is full of longing—you could have found out," Lynn said roguishly

Being improper and informal was something both monarchs were thirsty for, and he let the situation be what it was. Grief, fear, and need had to have a release—and when he felt her lean her forehead against the top of his shoulder, he knew it was not hot rain that fell against his bare skin. "You are still beautiful, Empress, and you deserve a mate who sees that. Perhaps in time, yours will wake up—before he loses everything he has ever loved and fought for. And M'lady, you are worth fighting for."

And then he kissed her temple amid the cry of ibises and the fast-growing frog chorus—and she smiled as she bit back a sob. "I want to feel alive," she whispered. "I'm not dead yet."

"I assure you, you are very much still alive. Walk with me when the rain stops? If I remember correctly, there is an ancient temple nearby, and I'd greatly enjoy visiting it."

"Yes, but how do you know?" The empress sounded mystified.

"It was on one of her old maps, I memorized them when I was a boy."

Sarah was grateful for the mundane nature of her problems. Stubbing out her cigarette, she turned to give Rose a welcoming smile. "Finished making our prince's potions?" she teased, patting the ammo crate beside hers.

"Made them long ago and sent them with him. That should help improve his outlook on life," she said.

"You know, in all this time, I wouldn't have known if Grayden hadn't told me." Sarah frowned. "What's it like, being a healer and handling that sort of request?" Being an ex-bartender in Sine had taught her a thing or two, and she had seen men and women at the highest and lowest; but how did a healer handle requests like Brynn's… ethically?

Rose shook her head, full lips turning up into a warm smile. "I do it because it's the right thing to do. The right thing for him, too. Sometimes things happen, and it's not my place to judge. From what I understand, he wasn't happy as he was before, and I wouldn't have been, either. Can you imagine someone calling you 'he' every waking minute of your day when you are definitely a 'she'? It doesn't matter what we think, or what parts our dear prince does or doesn't have. He's no different than you and me."

"Right," Sarah confirmed. "The excuse of 'it's the way it has always been done' isn't the truth, nor is it the answer. Brynn knew he was a man, the way I knew I never wanted to be with one."

"Correct." The healer wiggled her bandaged fingers with an uplifted eyebrow. "And… on that topic, and regarding the matter of your old fashioned cure… I do suppose my fingers feel better," Rose giggled huskily, a blush staining her high cheekbones.

"A little love can go a long way," Sarah said sagely, offering over the bottle of mead she had been taking sips from. She had hidden it behind the crates and been pulling it out to sip at it little by little. '*Mundane*,' she repeated in her head. Her problems, their problems, Brynn's problems… were mundane.

The rain was still pouring. There wasn't enough food or medical supplies again, and a case of the sniffles had been going around. The survivors were cranky and tired of being cramped up in a cave, so they were squabbling—it was normally leadership burden. Annoying, but there were far worse things in life.

"A little love? Is that what we're calling it, now?" Rose laughed. The time she and Sarah had stolen away to share hadn't been insignificant by any means, at least not to the healer. She then thought about Brynn and Tylen. Miles was with them, and they wouldn't be alone; but they were young. So very young, and while she wasn't one to judge— she wasn't exactly wizened herself—she still worried about them.

"That's what we're calling it," Sarah answered, raspy voice low as she tilted her head back against the wall behind her. "It seems so small, doesn't it? Love, in the midst of all this mess and violence. It seems like nothing by comparison, like if it isn't the right kind—or strong enough in the way we think it should be—it will be snuffed out. But you know…" She found herself looking back at Rose, meeting those wide green eyes. "There will always be war, and darkness, and hate. And you know what defeats it every time?"

Rose was riveted on Sarah's brown eyes, her mouth

a parted cupid's bow of silent "what."

"That little bit of love. Not blind love, not violent love, or passion, or passivity. Love that sees past fear, and prejudice. Finding love, that spark of happiness in all the darkness, and loving in the ways you can, and without thought of anything in return… that's what saves the day."

"Hope. You're telling me love is hope."

"Yep," Sarah grinned, her head turning lazily against the wall until she could press her lips to Rose's— and the healer's bandaged fingers found her short hair, twisting there as they shared a breath that tasted of mead.

"What is it?" Grayden asked Ella as he pushed his hood back from his soaking gray hair. She was staring into the peat-fire, her numb hands raised to it as the Cideshii couple beside her watched on—multi-faceted eyes glittering in the firelight.

Vix and Donovan had been accepted into another dwelling for the night so the small hut wouldn't be overcrowded. Cideshii housing didn't smell nice, and it was congested by the mage and tracker's presence—but it was warm, and Grayden appreciated warm.

"It sounds frivolous in my head, Archmage. I don't feel inclined to share it," Ella replied—pushing her dripping braid back behind her shoulder.

"Humor an old man," Grayden grimaced, rubbing his hands together. Thank goodness Cideshii were exothermic and required more heat than most to keep from falling into a state of hibernation. He didn't feel far from it himself, his aching leg so stiff he wasn't able to sit without fear he might not be able to stand again.

"Grayden..."

"Ella..." He gave her a tired but impish grin, and she relented, shaking her head.

"I miss Miles. There. Are you happy?"

"Aha! I thought so!" Grayden crowed, starling the nearby Cideshii farmer and his mate. "Sorry, sorry," Grayden patted the air apologetically until the couple's eye stalks stopped quivering. It had upset them enough to have dragons landing out in their field, but to catch sight of a man who had been reported missing—let alone have him as a guest in their hut—had rattled them more than they let on.

"There's something else," Ella said softly. "But I'll tell you later." Her hand paused over her belly worriedly before she moved to take off her cloak, and Grayden's eyes widened.

"You have got to be kidding me," he hissed, catching her wrist, turning her to look at him. She was as tall as him, and she met his eyes fiercely enough that he reconsidered what he was about to say. "Does Miles know?" he asked lamely.

The insects beside them were increasingly lost in the drama they were witnessing, even if they had no idea what was being discussed. They were farmers and couldn't afford to be schooled in Anteas' languages.

"I'm here, aren't I? What's there to know? I'm needed and I have work to do. It will be if it is meant to be. And if it's not, then Miles will never know, and you won't tell him."

"Ella..."

"Don't you 'Ella' me. I'm a grown woman who makes her own decisions—and don't even try that tired line about how it's 'half his decision'. My body, my decisions. We should have known better at our age but here we are." She gestured widely with her free hand, then stopped herself when she realized how riveted their audience was becoming. Without saying another word, she jerked her wrist out of Grayden's grasp and sat angrily beside the fire again—moving to stir the pot there. Their hosts had put on a vegetable soup for them, and she wouldn't let it burn because Cideshii were too culturally polite to interrupt.

Grayden sat heavily, his knee creaking ominously as he levered himself onto the dirty rug beside the fire. "Ella..."

"Grayden!"

"I wasn't going to argue. I was going to congratulate you." He had also been about to light a cigarette, but now he had decided to abstain. "Don't die, okay? Miles is a good man, and you've brightened up his life. The thing you're talking about, he's wanted that for a long time, too. Do you?"

That gave the tracker pause. "I never even thought about what would happen when this war was over. I never thought I'd live to see peace."

"I don't think anyone ever does. I can't remember a time there wasn't war, but given my situation, I haven't had a chance to back away, either. You, though... you can. You aren't a soldier."

"What if I hit that right back at you, Archmage? If we live, what do you want to do?"

Grayden paused to give the struggling arkane heater by the door of the hut a smack—scoring a direct hit without looking, which made the machine cough back to life. "Do you know what I'd do, Ella? I think I'd finally quit."

This made the woman raise an eyebrow.

"I'd take a vacation with Lynn, put Brynn and his boyfriend in charge—don't look at me like that, they can't do worse at this rate. Oh, yeah, and you know what else I'd do?"

He tugged down the edge of his tunic to reveal his brand. Ella took in a sharp breath, but he ignored it. "I'd have Lynn rip up my service papers, and ask one of the local healers to cut this puppy off—I'd walk away a free man. I think I'd buy some land somewhere nice, and make myself a little farm before I'm too old to do it. And I would never. Ever. On pain of death. Sign another requisition form again."

Ella laughed abruptly, some of the tension leaving her shoulders as she bowed her head over the pot to hide her smile. "So you figured out you were being put out to pasture, eh?"

"How could I not." He let the fabric slide back into place at his shoulder.

"It sounds like a good change, if you ask me."

"What about you?"

"I want to retire. Maybe I'll even take Miles off your hands."

"You had best, Ella. That man needed a reprieve from duty fifteen years ago, and in the most positive sense. He has done hard time."

"You mean *Broderick* time?"

"He deserves to raise a family of his own," Grayden said.

"We'll see," Ella replied, accepting a bowl from one

of their hosts. The Cideshii family was so poor they only owned one, so the two humans would share the dish.

"We will, won't we?" Grayden asked.

"Stop worrying, Archmage. You're making your wrinkles worse."

Grayden snorted in reply, looking away into the fire. "Eat your fill, I'll finish what's left."

"I'm not going to break, Grayden."

He didn't answer her, letting his head drop into his hand. His plans had just gotten a whole lot more complicated.

Chapter Fourteen

rynn's heart was pounding so loudly he was surprised that Tylen couldn't hear it. Luckily, the prince was good at faking sleep—which had allowed him to overhear everything. He had also been perfectly aware when Tylen had lifted the key from his pocket. He should have been angry; he should have felt betrayed. Instead, he was worried about what might happen to the other boy.

Tylen was sincere, he believed what he was doing was right, and Brynn respected that. The dragon was taking terrible chances if he was a Separatist spy, and that helped Brynn to see past his initial assumptions. He had spent enough time in Tylen's quiet company to know that still waters ran deep, and that there was far more to him than met the eye—so that was what Brynn decided to put faith in: the good in Tylen. He might have had an awful family, but he wasn't lying when he said he loved Brynn.

Binding his chest quickly, the prince dressed and slipped into his cloak. Clipping his dagger to his utility belt and putting his compass in his tunic pocket, he took stock of the room to make sure he hadn't forgotten anything. He wasn't fully awake, but he was determined not to leave anything they might need behind. He also couldn't afford to get caught.

If Miles found out what Brynn was planning, he would never let him go again; so on his way out, the prince scanned the hall for the night guard first—and was careful to hold the door just-so in the frame to keep the hinge from creaking. Wherever Tylen was going, he was in danger, and Brynn wouldn't let him face that alone. If that meant sneaking out of the barracks of Helith in beastly weather... then so be it.

The night was bright, like walking in a lamp-lit city, and the moon was full and silver over the wet sands, lighting the bright white of melting snow in the distant mountain range. Far off, a heron called, and frogs and crickets that hadn't been drowned called stridulously for mates. Heat lightning flashed, a crocodile bellowed, and somewhere a desert fox yipped. The land was alive, and all but vibrating with the intensity of life thundering into bloom; but Lynn was merely an observer. His heart ached to reach out, to heal and enjoy, but he felt he had no right when his people suffered—and when the Angelic were about to destroy Anteas as they knew it.

The king's boots made deep tracks as he strode through the twilight, the weight of the world on his shoulders… while the empress beside him left bare footprints—the difference between the marks on the land erasing themselves as the indentations filled with inky water; the stars reflecting equally in each footstep.

The two moved in silence, the smell of night-blooming jasmine heady around them. The way Lenna was studying Lynn reminded him that he was not a dragon, and she was not human—but he wasn't uncomfortable with that. If anything, it was reassuring. She wasn't the sort to try her hand at platitudes.

Before them, the white sandstone pillars of an open temple thrust skyward like bones in an oasis, and Lynn paused. Touching his thumb and forefinger to his forehead, he allowed himself to remember his mother, his late wife, and their son.

Lenna stopped beside him. "Do you want to see them?" she asked, her voice breathy, even though their pace hadn't been rushed.

"See them?" Lynn asked curiously. "I could do that?"

"I can share my memories of your mother with you.

It is a small thing, but this is the perfect place and time for it."

"Why would you do that? I have nothing to give you in return," Lynn asked, expression open and honest in the low light.

"You have nothing that I want to take, human. Not even your life. But as a dragon, I can do something you cannot. I can call upon the memories of the earth, and the echoes of all the stories woven into the tapestry of life... and show them to you."

"Flight memory. It's like racial memory... isn't it? I've heard of it, but I assumed it was some sort of magic. Human science can't explain it."

"All of those who are conceived in the dust of the cosmos can do what dragons do. That includes humans, in case you were wondering. Dragons just haven't forgotten how," Lenna said. "In some ways, my people are much less complicated than humans. We feel more deeply and simply, so we compensate with a great deal of introspection."

"It does make you the perfect stewards."

Lenna shook her head at that, striding forward while raising her hand high. She grazed her fingertips along a pillar, and a shimmering blue-violet light rose up from the stone to greet her—as eager as a kitten arching its back to be stroked.

"So your dead are never truly dead, just like ours. The dragon this temple was built for—his energy has leeched into every inch of this ground as his body went back to the earth—and I can read his memories if I reach out," Lenna turned to offer her other hand to Lynn. "Come. Do you want to see? This is not something we offer to many mortals, Lynn Broderick, Son of the Desert."

"I can ask to see anything, or anyone that you have a memory of?"

"Yes, Lynn. You can."

Around the king, the night air thrummed with arkane power, the ground beneath their feet shivering with it… and Lynn nodded. What was a once in a lifetime chance not taken?

The rain was alternating between peaceful pattering and outright cloudbursts, and the forest south of Helith was terrifyingly dark when the rainfall was at its heaviest. Sometimes the moon would come out from between the scudding clouds—and that was when Brynn would catch sight of Tylen and scurry to catch up. The dragon was following something that human eyes could not see, and Brynn did not question.

They were moving steadily away from the fort, at least, that was what the prince's compass told him when flashes of moonlight allowed him to read the face. He had lost track of how long he had been out in the forest, focusing only on Tylen's rust colored cloak weaving in and out of the clawing bracken. Brynn had stubbed his toes too many times to count—and fallen at least a dozen more— yet he had managed to keep silent enough to avoid drawing the dragon's attention. It also didn't hurt that Tylen was fixated on whatever he was pursuing to the exclusion of everything else.

Staggering up a muddy mountain foothill, clinging to tree trunks with wet, numb fingers, the prince inched forward until he could kneel behind some nearby undergrowth. Before him, a massive clearing in the woods had opened up, and in the center of it stood Tylen... and a slight young woman with bright silver hair. She didn't seem to mind the rain, and wore no cloak. There was something otherworldly about her, and Brynn knew without being told that she and Tylen were related—and that meant that it could only be one person.

"Lukka!" Tylen shouted over the rain, his voice sharp and commanding despite the renewed fury of the storm above them.

The downpour was growing warmer, and thunder

rolled—the front had come directly from Tel'aven, and it smelled of ocean salt and the musk of damp desert sand; at least, that was what Brynn thought. That, or Tylen's sister was some sort of conjurer, and she had found a way to bring the magic of her home with her.

"You needn't have worried. I brought it," Tylen said—or Brynn thought that was what he said. Trying to read Tylen's lips in low light wasn't easy, nor was straining his ears past the strike of rain on naked tree branches and frozen earth.

The young woman's reply to Tylen was impossible to make out; but Brynn's attention was mostly drawn by the way she moved. Like an adder through marsh water, she wound her way to Tylen, her fingertips tracing the rainwater on his face. Everything she did seemed designed to make Brynn jealous, and his stomach knotted tightly. What right did she have to touch anyone in such a manner—especially a relative!

"You brought it for *me*? Lukka whispered, standing so close that her lips were only a hair's breadth away from Tylen's.

He could taste the rainwater on her skin, and the hint of blood from her last kill—it had been recent, and it was bitter, stinking of human. She was killing and eating people; and Tylen wondered who it had been this time; his stomach giving a rebellious lurch. "I didn't bring it for you. I will give it to *them* myself." He stepped back sharply from her touch, breathing shallowly through his nose to avoid vomiting.

Her expression changed briskly from one of coquettish hopefulness to outright disgust. "Weak! You are weak. They will destroy you for your troubles. You always were too soft to take Mother's place. What makes you think the Angels will let you live after they have taken the key from you? They've drained every last Half-dragon dry!"

"Not *every* Half-dragon, Lukka," Tylen left the accusation of their heritage unspoken. "But in case you were worried about me—and I know you aren't—I don't intend to come back. That should be good news for you and Father, shouldn't it?"

That brought Lukka up short, and Tylen could see her recalculating her trajectory. She wouldn't have any power without him, and she knew that. Well, she *could*, but she would have to work far harder that way than if he cooperated.

"Poor, simple Tylendros. Give the key to me, and I will spare you such a fate. All your suffering will be over if you come to me." Her hands slipped down the curves of her chest and belly, and Tylen made the mistake of watching them instead of staring straight ahead.

She moved fast, and striking like a snake she caught his face in both her hands—and Tylen recoiled, backing away. "Don't touch me!" he snapped. Normally he didn't acknowledge or reject her advances because it would only encourage her. She was a bully, and she always had been.

"You don't want me? You'd rather mate with a human than me? Tylen... what would Father say?"

The awkward position of Lukka's footing on the muddy ground betrayed her; and when she reached out to Tylen and he jerked back again, he tripped her and himself—ending up on one knee in the muck as she went sprawling. "Don't touch me!" he snapped hotly.

"Prickly today, aren't we?" she crooned from where she'd fallen onto her hip—her tone was sweet, but there was no hiding the hate in her eyes.

As they both stood, Lukka regarded Tylen coldly. With mud staining her hands from her fall, she reached out a third time, ignoring his attempts at escape—and as her fingertips brushing his jaw, that was when there was an explosion of arkane magic, and Tylen wasn't in human form anymore.

"What do I do?" Lynn asked, voice reverent and barely audible over the din of the desert night. He could feel Lenna behind him, the soft curves of her body pressed against his back. He had since put his dry tunic on, but it might as well have been non-existent and both of them bare. Her touch was so… intimate—and in a way that his contact with other dragons hadn't been. He suspected that was part of who she was, and her own unique brand of magic—which was almost sexual, but not quite—and he would be lying if he said he didn't feel the chemistry between them.

"All you have to do is say her name, and picture something about her that you remember most clearly. The rest will happen. It's like turning a key in a lock," Lenna replied, taking Lynn's hands in hers, and raising them up over his head toward the nearest pillar. "Go on," she whispered, watching the glow building around the stonework. The earth, and dragon-kind, had not forgotten the children of the desert.

In retrospect, Lynn wouldn't even remember whispering his mother's name. He wouldn't remember Lenna's soft lips brushing the shell of his ear, or the way it felt like their hearts beat in time. All he would recall was her guiding his hands until his fingertips touched stone, and blinding white light… Then he was a boy again, and watching his mother walk the limestone docks of Tel'aven.

Pausing at the water's edge, she scooped up a lotus flower; her brown, elegant hands breaking it free of its leaves and stem to tuck it into her braids. Despite the difficult curation of natural hair, she had always grown hers long; and regardless of the intricate ties, bands, and coils that wove in and out of braided sections, it was forever as untamed and full of life as the woman herself. When she looked up to him—seeing him, but not seeing him—he was reminded again of where he had inherited his eye color. Their eyes, his and hers, were darker than honey, but neither brown nor gold.

Her other gift to him had been the freckles over the bridge of her nose. She had often sunburned as a child playing along the Tel'av river—a thing which she told him of when applying aloe to his inevitable burns as a boy—and as strange as it was, he took comfort from those memories of her. He had been teased for the marks blooming along his skin when he was small—not dark enough to fit in among his mother's people, but assuredly too dark for his father's kin. According to legend, freckles indicated not fitting into either world; but his mother had worn hers as a badge of courage. She had feared nothing. No man, dragon, or beast could avoid her friendship, and all truths could and would be known when she was involved.

She had always roamed the land unfettered and fearless of consequence. No part of the desert was unknown to her, and she had not been a sheltered princess. She believed in experiencing life—and he knew full well she had taken lovers before his father. That knowledge was only reaffirmed when he realized the way that his mother was smiling was not for him—but for Lenna.

Younger, lither Lenna. And he watched the two of them join hands and walk down the docks to watch the sunrise. His heart skipped a beat. And then another. There were tears streaming down his face. To see his mother alive again, light and carefree away from the grief that had taken her from him—to know she lived on in such a capacity, even if it was within an echo in a dragon's memories… it made him believe she wasn't completely gone. And suddenly he felt less alone.

If he concentrated, he could feel the cramp in his knees from where he stood, still as a statue reaching up to bind himself and Lenna to the earth as they explored the past. He could smell jasmine, and feel the feather-warm brush of desert winds tamed by rain. But he didn't want to. He wanted to live a while longer. He wanted to remember what it felt like when he was full of reckless abandon, and every moment had been a joyous adventure. He wanted to remember his mother, and Lenna, the same.

"Welcome home, King Broderick. Welcome back to your heart. Your other half will join you soon," Lenna whispered, her words barely filtering through into his waking memory. He almost pushed them away, ignoring them as his thirsty heart drank in life and light... but he didn't. Because he knew he would have to return soon, and she was his only lifeline.

Sun and moon faced each other down between flashes of heat lightning and the grumble of thunder. Lukka's slighter Draconic form glowed silver in the dark, while Tylen's scales pulsed like a golden beacon. He had fed recently and recovered some of his vibrancy—his strength, on the other hand, was questionable, and Brynn was as awed as he was terrified. The prince couldn't think about being betrayed or angry—he could only focus on the fact that he didn't want to lose another person that he loved. "Don't do it!" he shouted, dashing out into the center of the clearing.

In hindsight it was a non-specific thing to shout. Don't do what? Don't give her the key? Don't give in? Don't fight her? Even Brynn didn't know as he stood knock-kneed before the two dragons. It also gave Lukka the opening she was looking for.

With Tylen's attention diverted to Brynn, the young queen reared back and struck, her fangs sinking into the joint where wing met shoulder.

For an instant, one golden eye met Brynn's pleadingly, but then it closed in pain as Tylen bellowed—whipping around to face his sister, shaking her fangs loose as he sidestepped her attack. The motion forced her to put her front feet down or risk falling, and gave Tylen the chance to gain traction while putting himself between her and Brynn.

"Run," Tylen said commandingly—blood trickling down his withers and turning his wet mane shades of gold-gilt pink. "Run, Brynn."

Brynn was shaking with adrenaline, but he didn't draw his dagger. Instead he rested one small hand against the heaving bulk of Tylen's side. "No. We face this together. That is the only way we will survive."

Lukka didn't seem impressed by Brynn's bravery, but she did take the second advantage she had been given. With a hiss she swiped with her front foot, her talons raking down Tylen's side—and his scales parted beneath their razor sharpness. Gold furrows fountained open along the drake's side, and all patience was lost.

Throwing himself into Lukka chest first, Tylen slammed all of his weight into his sister's slighter form, sitting her firmly down on her backside in the mud—and before she could gain her feet again, he whipped around and lashed her with his tail. The impact was so explosive that it sounded like lightning striking the earth, and her front legs went out from under her fast enough to pitch her onto her face and send her sliding in the mud.

"Leave me!" Tylen snarled, watching with no small amount of satisfaction as she skidded through the muck and struck a tree. His fangs were bared, and his neck frills were flared as he watched his sister struggle to right herself. His every motion was intimidating—a nearly grown male utilizing every bit of his size and shape for a threat display. He wasn't ready to kill her, but he wanted nothing to do with her, either.

Lukka, on the other hand, didn't back down when she should have. She had tasted first blood, he had broken her leg in retaliation, and common sense wasn't her strong suit when she was furious.

Rising on her three good limbs, her wings crooked for balance, Lukka clutched her broken foreleg to her chest. "How *dare* you," she whispered coldly, her human voice lost to the Draconic power surging within her.

Tylen stood bodily between Brynn and his sister's

wrath, and the desperation in his posture could not be missed. Impressive, if bleeding and broken, he intended to give a good account of himself. In his flight, it was rare that a drake stood up to a queen, let alone attacked her; but he had no choice. Lukka was a murderer, and he wouldn't let her take Brynn, too.

Smoke trickled from Tylen's nostrils as he watched Lukka draw the arkane around herself like a shield—and he knew what she was planning. Arkane users could utilize a shield to protect themselves, then detonate it like a bomb in instead of letting it naturally dissipate. Tylen would survive such a close-quarters maneuver because he was trained to, he could shield himself while absorbing some of the arkane power into himself. But he couldn't do that while protecting Brynn at the same time—that required more finesse than an inexperienced young mage owned. Thus, it was Tylen's increasing desperation that finally drove him to do something he had never done before; something which he had never let himself do, even as a dragonling when it was normal for such behaviors to develop—he breathed fire.

The gout of flame was enormous, pushing back the darkness and blinding everyone on the ground—Tylen included—and it ripped through Lukka's shield before it could peak in power. The young queen lost her grip on the remaining energy she had been raising, and the spell turned back on her at the same time the flames reached her silver scales. She went sprawling again—this time into the tree behind her, shearing it off at ground level. She was enveloped in fire and arkane energy as she rolled in the snow and mud, trying to put herself out amid the rain of bark, chunks of tree-trunk, and branches.

Tylen's attention never left his opponent as he waited for his night-vision to return—his head lowered, his muzzle almost touching the ground. As he panted for breath, mouth gaping and beard scales darkened, he felt like something inside of him had broken open; and he considered his sister as she went still on the far side of the clearing. Would she come at him again, or had he won?

For an instant after she collapsed, Lukka looked like she might try to get up and fight; but the pain of her burns caught up with her, and she rose to her feet with a trumpet of pain… then ran. She scampered away as best she could on three legs—and Tylen let her go, hopelessness building in the pit of his stomach. She hadn't gotten a chance to out him to Brynn, but if he didn't tell the other boy sometime soon, she would—and she would be back, he could feel it in the pit of his stomach. Mind, that was assuming the prince would ever speak to him again after all this. Were he in the other boy's position, he probably wouldn't have wanted anything to do with someone like himself.

Behind him, Tylen could hear Brynn's unsteady approach through the mud, but he couldn't bring himself to look at him for shame. All he could see was his own reflection, and his mane pooling in the puddles beneath him as blood dripped—blooming golden in the inky, churned water.

"Did you hear that?" Grigor asked, pressing his back flat against the slime encrusted wall behind him. He'd stopped dreaming about baths two days prior, and now he just wanted to survive.

Sevaren crouched in the shadows, the crimson glow of his eyes the only color in a world long forgotten and drained of life. "I did," the dragon admitted.

The softest tread of footsteps echoed uncertainly, then stopped.

They were being followed. Chell had caught sight of their hunters once—four of them, dressed wildly and wearing abandoned pieces of old world detritus. They looked nothing short of fanatical, and it went unspoken that if any of the rogue's group had a choice between suicide and capture, they were wise to choose suicide.

"This way," Chell said sternly, her curly hair

plastered to her sweaty skin. She was as tired and filthy as the rest of her companions—and the game of survival was growing more difficult by the minute. It had been noted time and again that getting into Ambis was hard, but getting out was almost impossible; and Chell was cursing herself for thinking she could do better the second time around. She had most likely doomed her companions to a horrible death—and for a futile mission at that.

Hearing low, muttering voices, she pulled Loux closer to her side. The other woman was constantly overwhelmed by the emotional leavings of the culture that Ambis was built upon—and she had devolved to needing someone to lead her over the last few hours. She was also the only one carrying the map—which she refused to relinquish—and Chell would not let her fall behind. "This way," she murmured, gesturing to a tunnel heading the opposite direction of the voices. She was starting to recognize minor details—this was the way they had come in, she was sure of it.

"Holy shit," Brynn spluttered when he managed to find words again. Picking his way across the impromptu field of battle, he hit his knees in front of Tylen, taking that overheated muzzle into both his hands. The dragon's golden eyes were closed, and a croon of abject grief left him as Brynn pressed their foreheads together. "Tylen... are you alright?"

Tylen tried to lift his head, to pull back from Brynn's touch, but his legs were too shaky. "I'm fine. You should go."

Brynn frowned at that, sitting back. "Look at me," he demanded, even though he was trembling, too. "I said look at me!" He gave Tylen's snout a gentle slap, and gold eyes fluttered open—a smack to scales wasn't as painful for a dragon as it was for a human.

There was such regret and hurt in the dragon's visage, but he seemed to be trying to focus on Brynn instead of losing himself to his misery. "That's better. I don't know why you thought this was a good idea, Tylen, but I also do. Don't think I'm not angry, because I am—and I assure you we will discuss this later. You're an idiot, and apparently I am too, but I love you and we're going to face this together. If you think we should take the key to the Angelic, then *we'll* do it. And if we die, we die hand in hand. I'm not losing one more person I care about, Tylen. Not today, not ever."

Tylen should have said something, anything, and he wanted to—but he was in too much pain to do more than carefully press his snout into Brynn's chest, hiding his eyes and nostrils beneath the soggy sanctuary of the other boy's cloak.

"Also… that was kind of incredible. How did you do that? The… breathing fire thing."

Tylen shifted his position uncomfortably, swallowing the words he wanted to say. The fact that Brynn wasn't terrified of dragons after what he had just witnessed, well, it was enough to make Tylen believe he had underestimated the prince in more than one way. The fact that Brynn wasn't irate about the betrayal of trust and theft of the key was also an outright miracle—which Tylen wouldn't turn his nose up at. Yes, he believed Brynn; they would be having a heavy discussion sooner rather than later. But they were alive, and Lukka was gone, so it was time to head back to the barracks.

"Come," Tylen sighed out heavily, fighting the urge to apologize or make excuses; they didn't have time for that. "There is no way that scuffle went unnoticed by the sentries back at Helith—we aren't that far away. Let's fly back before they decide to come after us. I don't know how far Lukka will retreat to lick her wounds, or who she's going to report to; but she knows we're in Helith, so we should move quickly. She's angry… very angry."

Brynn frowned. "It's way too late for any of that, Tylen, it doesn't even make sense to worry. If she already knows where we are, it's safe to say Baron Forscyth does, too. Am I wrong? To say this is a huge mess is an understatement."

"No. You're right. I know she knows too much. But let me fly you back anyway. There's safety in numbers right now."

"Fly me? In your condition?" Brynn looked at the blood trickling from the base of the dragon's wing and dripping down his sides. "Why don't you shift back and let me help you? You gave Lukka a beating and she will stay away long enough for us to walk back. Besides, the bleeding will slow if you're in human form. Maylin said dragons take mortal guise when they're hurt—you lose less blood and you heal faster when you expend less energy."

Tylen shook his head at that. Leave it to Brynn to be the only practical one between them. "Flying is faster, and it isn't that far. Let's not give my sister a chance to circle around and cut off our retreat."

"Would she?" Brynn made a show of trying to stop the bleeding from a fang wound on the side of Tylen's neck—and only managed to dislodge half a tooth buried in the wound. He swallowed hard at Tylen's wince and the pained wrinkle of his muzzle.

"What do *you* think?" Tylen hissed.

Miles raised his hand to his brow, staring in the direction the sentries had reported smoke. The soldiers of Helith had built an observation tower from some of the leftover barn wood in the village center—and it was a bad night to be up on it. Lightning and rain were risks, but the commander needed to be able to see at distance.

"How long ago?"

"Not even five minutes, Sir," the mage sentry replied.

"And you saw arkane fire as well as a gout of flame?"

"Yessir. Several trees were knocked over, too. We don't have enough rough terrain around us to miss something that major."

The night watch was a mage, and Miles trusted his expertise. "Should we put together an investigation team?" he asked, his tone weary. He had been jerked out of bed when one of the hall guards had discovered that Tylen and Brynn missing. The commander was beginning to paint a picture in his head, one that he didn't particularly like the color of.

"I would, sir. We already have one of the guerrilla teams ready to head to Skyeford. We could reroute them."

"Sounds like an excellent idea. Let me know what you find out, and as soon as you can."

"Yessir."

It had been hell for Brynn to find a position he was comfortable in that didn't hurt Tylen, and takeoff had been shaky at best—but they were finally in the air now, and the storm had descended on them with full fury.

Copelan had survived a similar flight because he was a bigger dragon. He was done growing, and his weight and mass had given him far more stability in the air. Tylen, was younger, wounded, less experienced at flight—let alone carrying a passenger—and the weather was, in Brynn's estimation, the worst to fly in yet. He and Tylen were being hammered by alternating updrafts and downdrafts, and neither of them could see properly for the rain… then the hail had started.

Brynn had managed only one peek at his compass since their flight had taken a downward turn—and it had been furtive, backlit only by heat lightning that made the hair on his arms stand on end. Lightning also made it hard for him to tell if the compass was accurate; but if the glance he had gotten was truthful, they were headed east instead of north. The wind had turned them, and there was nothing for it. Tylen was in no condition to fly headlong into the wind to correct their course. "Put down! Tylen we have to put down and wait this out!"

He could feel the shaking of Tylen's muscles. The drake was exhausted, and for the first time Brynn's feeling of dread morphed to outright fear. They could very well fall from the sky and die, and for what? They were now further from the Helith than when they started.

"Can't!" Tylen shouted back over the wind. "We have to keep going!"

That was when Brynn realized that all he could see was dark water beneath them. They were being forced out over tempest-driven East Ocean, and there was nowhere for Tylen to land at all. "Shit," the prince muttered darkly to himself.

"Do you ever disgust yourself?" The Baron asked the dragon before him.

The young queen was dripping rainwater on the floor, her broken arm clasped tightly to her chest. Her shoulder on the side of the break was badly burned, and the blisters crawling up her neck stopped just shy of her jaw. She was shaking in outrage and pain. "He has the key," she replied dully, as if that was the proper answer all along.

"And now he's aware that I know where the survivors are hiding, you absolute imbecile!" The Baron threw the book he had been reading across the room where it thumped to a stop against a marble pedestal—spine down, pages fluttering futilely.

"Are you listening to me?" The queen hissed between chattering teeth. "He has the key; all you have to do is retrieve it! Nothing else matters."

"Then what use are you? I can't just up and do your bidding! I am your master, Lukka, and I am disappointed. Very disappointed. I hired you to do this work for me, and now you are suggesting I should do it myself?" The Baron stood brusquely—then menacingly descending the steps that separated the reading room from the rest of the library. "You are a coward, and you stink," he hissed, face inches from Lukka's. "Get out of my sight. You have no idea what your failure has cost me."

Despite asking her to leave, it was he that strode from the room, leaning heavily on his cane. He walked like a man on a mission, and Lukka watched him depart with a dull, if feral, interest. "Maybe I do, Baron. Maybe I do, and you played directly into my game. I hope you get what you deserve," she muttered.

"I can't go on!" Tylen cried as the storm spat them out. The change from the cold, battering fury of the last hour was stunning. The sun was rising over the patchwork of rolling Tel'aven deserts and mountain ranges, and the air around them had gone from frigid to balmy.

Brynn was barely clinging to consciousness he was so cold, and his first coherent thought was a wry one. At least they would die warm. The beat of Tylen's wings was faltering, and he could feel the way the dragon's muscles were stiffening beneath his thighs—especially around the elbow on Tylen's wounded side.

They were in a downward spiral, Tylen trying to slow himself as best he could with a body that would not cooperate.

Brynn clung all the tighter as the coastal mountain range rushed up at them—no longer worried about Tylen's comfort as much as he was not being thrown off. A wing connected with the tip of a stony peak, shearing off a chunk of rock as Tylen tried to find an updraft to give him some loft—and the jarring impact through the dragon's body made the other boy clench his teeth in pain. "Over the mountains, we have to make it over the mountains!" Brynn called as Tylen bellowed his hurt.

A water landing would be lethal; with was no coast, only cliff face—thus no way out of the ocean—the surf would batter them against the base of the mountains until they drowned. No. Brynn was determined that they would have to attempt a ground landing, for better or for worse.

"Easy for you to say!" Tylen shouted back, adjusting his pitch and backwinging again as he found an updraft current.

Easy indeed, Brynn thought. They were still circling downward too fast; but the support of the upwelling of hot air had given Tylen a moment of relief that let dragon and passenger study the tapestry of land before them.

The first rains had come and gone, and the sands were sodden and sparkling; and as the duo lost enough altitude, Brynn could see the thick papyrus blooms choking the overfilled rivers that dotted the land.

"Hold tight!" Tylen shouted as the ground continued to rush up at them.

The last thing Brynn remembered was an explosion of sand and shale, and being thrown from Tylen's back—then darkness.

rayden was leaning against an arkane crawler, lighting his second cigarette of the morning. The night had passed quickly for him, but the memories of how hot and cramped it had been lingered. It reminded him of a time long gone, and before he had been sold. He needed space.

Ella was doing her best to act insulted with him for going outside to smoke. He had told her that not everything was about her, and that their Cideshii hosts were sensitive to the chemicals in cigarettes—but more than anything, he was concerned about her health and the child she was carrying. He was concerned about her, full stop.

Peering out over the melting, snow covered fields, he bit back another sigh when someone lean stepped up beside him. Of all the people he thought might seek him out, he had not been expecting Donovan.

"Spare me the whole 'what do you need, Rogue,' speech, okay?" the other man sighed.

Grayden nodded his head gamely, and then moved

over.

Leaning back against the strut of the crawler, Donovan held out his hand. "Bum a smoke?" he asked.

"Didn't know you smoked."

"I do today. Starting now," Donovan said.

"You shouldn't, it's a filthy habit," Grayden admitted.

"Listen. About that..." The rogue took the offered cigarette and lighter.

"I already know about Ella, if that's what you're going to tell me."

"Aww, naw, not that, mate," Donovan said as he flicked the lighter, then choked on his first drag. "What I was gonna tell you is, *I know*."

"You know what?" Grayden said. This was getting more and more interesting by the moment.

"They use these things to water the entire field," the rogue said, knocking on the metal pipe he was leaning against. "They're like a long chain on wheels, and arkane energy powers the engines that make them run. The crawlers don't mess up the rows while the plants in them are growing. First class stuff," Donovan said.

The seeming change in topic only briefly baffled Grayden. He knew how arkane crawlers worked. His family had been poor. He had played in the water on hot summer days before he had been shuffled off and sold. "That's not what you were going to say."

"No. It wasn't," Donovan said tiredly. "Look I'm not good with words, so I'm just going to say it. It's fuckin' brave of you to do this. You're playing decoy. I know you wouldn't have brought a pregnant lady if you'd had the first clue. You know you probably won't be coming back from this. You left what we needed behind with the kids, didn't you?"

Grayden smiled down at his cigarette, taking a last drag before he stubbed it out and field stripped it. He didn't intend to answer one way or the other. "And still, you came with me."

"Yeah, because Doc needs your help."

"You think *you're* coming back from this little jaunt?" The archmage asked.

"Does anyone? Every day you take your chances, but staying hidden doesn't necessarily better them."

"Then I guess you answered that question for yourself, didn't y..." Grayden paused—then looked up. "The hell is that?" he asked.

Donovan turned and peered north. "Smoke. I can see smoke. Way too much to be anything short of a massive fire."

Grayden frowned, looking away then. He had

suspected it was coming, but he had mixed feelings about it. He felt for the citizens; it wasn't their fault.

"No. Tell me that isn't Gent," Donovan groaned.

"When you play games you don't understand, you get burned," Grayden said softly.

"You knew this would happen?" The rogue turned to stare at Grayden, mouth open in shock.

Oh, how the tables had turned. "It wouldn't do any good to tell you that *I know*, now would it?" Grayden asked.

Donovan fell silent, his green eyes glued to the horizon and the plume of smoke. Absently, he took another drag, then had to turn away as he gave himself a second coughing fit.

"Lighter," the archmage demanded, holding his hand out expectantly.

The rogue placed the piece of cold metal back in the center of Grayden's palm, and without another word, the archmage strode away—heading back toward the huts, and the hum of Cideshii concern that was hovering in the air.

Rose sat hard, staring up at the sky above the tree line. The scout was kneeling and holding tight to his horse's reins, the beast breathing harshly beside him. Sarah still had a hand on the man's shoulder, but she only had eyes for Rose.

This was a possible outcome that had been discussed, and as Grayden's lieutenant, they had covered it. Sarah understood desperation from her time in the bars of Sine. People frantic to keep their lives did stupid things. The Angels were not only desperate, they held no respect for anything. They weren't part of anything on this planet—even on a biological level. They had kept the Baron in their employ because he was the only one who could give them what they needed. When he hadn't delivered, his usefulness had ended.

She knew about the key. Grayden had finally divulged that information to her in the time before his departure. She knew he had given it to Brynn. If Gent was burning, that meant the Baron hadn't gotten hold of what he needed to stave off the Angelic; and for the moment, Brynn and Grayden were safe. The innocent citizens of Gent, though? That was another story. "I'm so sorry," she whispered to Rose.

Rose had tears in her eyes, but she refused to let them fall. "Don't be. If the people had realized their power and stood up against my father sooner, this would never have happened. They don't deserve this, any of this," the healer murmured as if reading Sarah's mind. "But it doesn't change that good men and women stood by and did nothing while my father destroyed all they held dear. The bastard let the Angelic corruption into our ranks—and into our seat in Parliament—unchallenged. We didn't do enough, and this is our wages."

"Don't say 'our'," Sarah said gently. "You and your brother fought in every way you possibly could without losing your lives. Alive, you got more chances to fight him."

"It's true," Rose said softly. "But it's very hard to feel it that way."

"It always is when it's your home. When it's the only place you've ever known, and now it's gone."

"There is one good thing to come from this," Rose said, wiping her eyes on her sleeve.

"And what is that?" Sarah asked honestly.

"It means my father has finally lost favor with my people, and a good deal of his support. If what is left of the city and our army turns on him and finishes him off, I won't cry. This is his doing, and every single person knows it. The Angels wouldn't have been roaming the streets without his permission. He hedged his bets for too long, and now he's finally had to tap out."

Sarah frowned. "There is that. But if there is one thing I've learned in my day, it's that a man with nothing left to lose is exceedingly dangerous. Your father doesn't even have his pride."

"Yes," Rose said, swallowing hard and taking a shuddering breath to get her emotions under control. "If he's alive, we have all made him desperate. And that does concern me." Above the tree line, the smoke continued to roil. Gent was a long way away from the Foothill camp, so the fire had to be vast to be seen so clearly. "Do you think Brynn is okay?" Rose asked hopefully.

"I know it," Sarah replied. "If Gent is burning, the Angelic don't have what they want."

"What does that have to do with Brynn?" Rose asked, knowing she was being told something without being told.

Sarah just smiled and shook her head, leaning down and pulling out a cigarette. She was certain that wherever Grayden was, he was doing the same. They had to play this game a little longer, and fate would see to the rest.

TBC

For updates on upcoming releases:

Twitter: https://twitter.com/_WarMage

Website: http://www.warmage.ca

Facebook: https://www.facebook.com/K.W.Leone

Email: therealwarmage@gmail.com

A Note from The Author:

If you enjoyed your read, please leave a review!

Reviewing helps us reach more readers, and allows

us to keep bringing you the content that you love.

We want to hear from you!

www.ingramcontent.com/pod-product-compliance
Lightning Source LLC
Chambersburg PA
CBHW020430030726
47495CB00006B/1737